Tulare Kings Writers

Presents

Tales from the Strip Mall

Edited by Judith Bixby Boling

These stories are works of fiction. Names, characters, places, and incidents either are the product of the authors' imaginations or are used fictitiously. Any resemblance to actual persons, living or dead, events, or locales is entirely coincidental.

Cover design by Sylvia Ross

DEDICATION

To Roger Boling
His idea became
this anthology

CONTENTS

ABOUT TULARE-KINGS WRITERS

Tulare-Kings Writers is a networking group open to writers and aspiring writers wishing to connect with other writers. During our monthly meetings, we discuss topics relevant to the literary arts, participate in flash fiction exercises, or practice reading aloud from our own books.

Members of Tulare-Kings Writers staff a bookstall, filled with out members' published works, at Arts Consortium in Visalia, California during First Friday Art Hop.

Tulare-Kings Writers meets monthlyat 10 AM on the third Saturday. Presently, we meet at Tulare County Library in Visalia, and invite you to visit our Facebook page to confirm the date and location.

Contact us at tualrekingswritersca@gmail.com

The Metaphysical Emporium
Happiness

By Janet LeBaron

Magda sat on the sofa in her shop, watching grey skies submerge the town into premature twilight. She felt as bitter as the freezing wind, now shredding the WELCOME flag she had hoisted with pride, so many years ago.

"Well, Baby." She stroked the sleeping dog's head, "No more cookies for us. Diabetes." The Cocker Spaniel heard one word. She had his attention.

"And the lease is up." *For me, too, she thought*. "You won't be getting your petting from the people anymore. We'll miss our friends, won't we?" she said, tweaking his ears.

"Oh, what the hell," she told Baby, whose gaze followed her hand as she took a vanilla wafer from the plate. He waited patiently, a bit of drool on his lip, as she broke the cookie and gave him half. "It's your favorite, huh? No use your missing out, just cause of me."

Baby devoured the treat, then cocked his head, listening.

He jumped and twisted in mid-air, paws now on the sofa back, staring intently out the window. She turned to look. A young man, hunched against the cold, walked toward them. His parka was thin, and the sole of one shoe had separated.

"That's not Brigit, silly." She checked the clock on the shelf. Her daughter was due in forty-five minutes.

Magda sighed. Nothing in the store was hers any longer. Every book and trinket had been sold, and the new owners would take possession tomorrow. She would go and live with Brigit. There was no alternative. Magda knew she was a burden to this daughter, who loved animals more than her outspoken mother.

"Bossy Brigit," Magda grumbled. She felt the profound and irretrievable loss of her freedom in that moment. "I wish…"

Suddenly, the neon window lights came on, startling the man now passing. He stopped, and Baby barked loudly, excitement shaking down to his stubby tail.

"Tsk, tsk," she clucked, sizing him up. "No hat, Baby. Looks like he hasn't a friend in the world." A small thought began to take shape in her mind. "Baby." The dog's attention turned, looking deep into her eyes. "What do you think? Is he the one, Baby? Hmmm?"

"Woof!" the dog responded. Baby could always read her mind. Magda smiled.

ॐ

Arthur jumped as the lime green lights blinded him. He stepped back. The words, 'Metaphysical Emporium' illuminated the store window, while throwing an eerie glow on the sidewalk. Where was he? He spun around, and did not recognize the street. At the crosswalk, the sign was covered in graffiti. "Shit!" His frosty breath affirmed his dilemma. It was nearly dark, he was cold, and he was lost. Utterly lost.

He turned again to the window, where two faces greeted him. One was the sweetest dog he'd ever seen. The other was a woman. Pink neon window lights reflected the word, 'Crystals,' across her face. She was waving him inside, and Arthur felt the relief of promised sanctuary. He did not hesitate. Warmth and companionship, now.

An antique bell announced his entry, and a kind voice said, "Howdy-do! Come on in, shut the door." He did as commanded, at once enveloped in the dusky aroma of incense. Sundown and candles cast shadows around the shop. He saw a small shape racing toward him, and bent down.

The dog was in Arthur's arms, licking all available skin. "Well, here's Baby, come to meet you," laughed Magda, still seated near the window. "He likes you already."

Arthur lifted and hugged the dog, bringing him back to the sofa. "He's a friendly sod, isn't he?"

"Sit here, beside me," invited Magda, patting the cushion.

Arthur sat, placing the wriggling dog on his lap. This small animal embodied unconditional love. Life should be like this, he thought. It was real. True. This was what he missed. "You call him Baby?"

"Yes, that's my Baby. He's a love bug." Magda paused, studying the young man. "And, he loves cookies."

With a chuckle, Arthur spotted and reached for a vanilla wafer. Baby was hopeful, but respectful. He looked from the cookie to Arthur's eyes for permission. "Here you go, Baby," was all that was needed. The treat was gone instantly, and Arthur laughed, delighted. "What a life! Food, home and love." He stifled a sigh.

"Are you having a rough time, dear?" asked Magda, reaching into a purse at her feet.

Now his laugh was rueful. "Rough! Ha! Rough isn't the half of it." He dropped his guard while the warmth of the dog's belly thawed his cold legs. "My life is shit."

Magda reached out her hand, holding money folded tightly. "Take this," she said.

"No, no," he protested, astounded by her generosity. "I can't take that, but thank you." Unwilling tears found an exit, dropping onto the dog's head, and covered quickly by his hand. "I'm just tired of life."

Magda placed the roll of bills on the table, and bent once again into her bag. "Well, how about something to warm your soul, then?" She lifted a flask and unscrewed it. "I keep it to help me through," and took a long swig. "Don't tell my daughter, she'll be here soon," she said, handing it to him.

Arthur smelled the contents. *Rum!* He swallowed the burning liquid. *Delicious.* He drank again, forgetting to return it to her.

Comfortable moments of silence passed. Arthur rhythmically stroked the dozing dog, and his mind retreated into a hypnotic peacefulness. He was jolted back with Magda's question,

"Want to try the Wish Paper?" she asked, pointing to the

shelf behind him.

"What's that?" he asked, turning to see a small box sitting by itself among the books for sale. "That?" he repeated, reaching for it.

"Yes, that's the Wish Paper," she said, accepting it. "You think of something you wish would come true, and set the paper on fire. Then you blow on it, gentle-like. Your wish travels on it, and it rises into the air. It disappears in smoke, and the wish will come true."

"What? No." Arthur knew when he was being had, and laughed derisively. "No way. It's not that easy." He took another swallow of rum, dribbling a bit. His tongue caught it, and unthinking, he wiped his cold, dripping nose on his sleeve. "Ha! You sell wishes? People believe it?" He could feel the effects of the rum, a gentle euphoria cascading over him.

Magda chuckled. She was feeling the magic warmth as well. "Well, why not give it a try?" she prodded, giving his arm a teasing, gentle poke. The jostle woke Baby, who yawned and regarded Magda through sleepy eyes. "What do you have to lose?" Magda asked.

Arthur watched, transfixed. Her fingers lifted and opened the paper. It was formed in the shape of a cylinder, inscribed with gold symbols. She placed the tube on top of the box, and raised a match. Meeting his eyes, Magda prompted, "Got your wish ready?" He nodded. She lit the match, and touched the flame to the paper. As it rose into the air, the paper was consumed, replaced by spiral of white smoke. "Blow!" she commanded, sending it via her breath toward him. He grasped the dog, and closed his eyes, blowing the smoke into Baby's nose, who promptly sneezed.

Brigit entered the store, blustery wind ripping the door from her hand, the bell clanging fiercely. "Mama!" She could not see into the dimly lit room, and called again, "Ho, Mama, are you here?" She saw the dog approaching, and scooped him up with delight. "How's Auntie's good baby puppy-wuppy, now?" she cooed, burying her face in the dog's fur. She put him down gently, and seeing a light on in the back kitchenette, walked toward it. "Mama?"

There, joyful and triumphant, stood her mother. She was at the counter, up on her tip-toes, her face in a half-eaten can of dog food.

"What are you doing?" Brigit yelled. Her mother dropped the can and sat on the floor, big eyes asking forgiveness. Horrified, Brigit knelt down, realizing something was very wrong. She held her mother's face, looking into her eyes for recognition. She was rewarded with a lick on her nose. With shaking hands, Brigit took out her cell phone and called her husband. Her mother gave a contented burp, resting her head on Brigit's shoulder, tongue trying to catch a morsel that remained on her chin.

❧

Watching from the doorway, sat Arthur. He vaguely remembered one woman, and the other woman whistled to him in a friendly way. He padded over, responding to her welcome, and had his head stroked gently. How nice that felt. He was aware of a difference about himself, in a general, contented way. He lay down, snuggling into the space between them. The younger woman had an arm around the one she thought was her mother, rocking and crooning to her softly. Arthur felt the calmness in the bonding, and knew all would be well.

☙

In the shop, a man's lanky body was sprawled, asleep on the sofa. A familiar voice, her daughter's voice, roused Magda awake. "Brigit!" she replied, with a low, raspy voice. What time was it? She stood up without difficulty, surprised at the painless freedom of movement. Everything looked familiar, yet some-how *she* was different. She felt light as a feather, and strong. Magda switched on a light, and the hand on the fixture was not hers. Stunned, she turned it off, dropping back onto the sofa, closing her eyes. She was dreaming. Or was it the rum? Her mind froze.

Minutes passed, and the ease of breathing allowed her heartbeat to slow. Magda's fearless, pragmatic nature asserted itself. She would face this situation. Eyes still closed, she touched the muscled arm, the lean hand. Magda reached to her face, feeling gaunt angles where pudgy roundness should be. A stubble. She laid her hands in her lap- *a man's lap!* Boney legs in pants, rather than swollen elderly thighs. Her opened eyes confirmed the change. *How had this happened?*

She forced her mind to stop reeling, by demanding it replay the afternoon point by point. The sad young man. The rum! The Wish Paper! With a gasp, she remembered her wish. To be young and strong. To have the freedom and power to choose a different life! To have the opportunities of youth, with the wisdom of an elder. To be... Arthur! She *was*

Arthur! Except that she was still herself. Her mind, her memories. Yes, his clothes, his hands. With greater curiosity, she explored this new body, complete in every aspect. "Ha!" she gave an amused snort. She got up, easily again, and walked to the antique mirror. Looking back was that rather plain young man- yet her soul, behind his eyes.

Where was *he*, then? She walked guardedly toward the back room, and was unprepared for the sight. Her daughter was on the floor with the dog, and--herself! Her body, old, fat and- with an instant insight- It was Baby! Baby in her body! Magda watched as *her* hand, under Baby's control, reached out stealthily for the can of dog food, putting it behind her back. Baby the dog, sneezing at just the right moment, had his wish fulfilled. He was finally in control of the food.

Before Magda could completely process this insight, another followed quickly. The dog had heard the sound of Magda's footstep, and lifted his head. Magda looked into his eyes, and it was Arthur looking back. He stared for five seconds, then gave a brief "Woof!" Arthur, now the Cocker Spaniel, buried his body closer against Brigit, embracing his new life. Magda understood. He would be loved as a cherished pet, forever cared for, responsibility free.

Her daughter, suddenly aware of a male stranger, screamed.

Magda leapt backward, knocking over a display in the store. She caught her balance, and instinctively bent to pick up a fallen brass Buddha. Seeing again *his* hand reach out, she stopped. Everything had changed. This was not her

Buddha, not her store, and not her life.   With a final glance, she saw her folded money on the table-the years of savings! Seven crisp one-thousand-dollar bills. With giant strides, Magda captured and stuffed the money into his tight, thin slacks. Brigit was shrieking with threats of police. Magda's instincts took over. She ran to the door and flung it wide. The wind hit her full force, wild and invigorating. She laughed, exultant, new air filling her lungs. Whatever was next would be better than what had been.

She was free.

Waggin' Tails
A Dog's Story

By Ronn Couillard

If you were to wander about the North Point Mall, chances are you would come upon an establishment known as Waggin' Tails. As the name would imply, this is a pet grooming establishment. It is a fairly profitable business—washing, brushing, and trimming dogs of all types, from unkempt mongrels to the most dainty of the breeds. They can change the mangiest of mutts into being totally presentable—sort of like Professor Higgins changing Eliza Doolittle in *My Fair Lady*.

Dorothy, the owner and operator, is a no-nonsense woman with a dour personality and lacking any noticeable sense of humor. It is rumored that someone once saw her smile, but that rumor remains unsubstantiated. Though not given to engage in conversation, when she does speak, one would think she is a drill instructor giving orders that had better be obeyed. Dorothy, who always dressed in a pair of black tights and a white smock, would best be described as a rather large woman. Tall and wide, she had forearms like a blacksmith. Atop this big body is a round, moon-shaped face, with ruddy cheeks and covered with hair that might be referred to as dish-water blonde.

Dorothy's size and dour personality, coupled with her lack of humor, makes for a most intimidating presence. But it is agreed by all, that despite this gruff exterior, she has a warm spot in her large heart for her canine customers. She is known to have a calming way with even the most unruly of them. But, if her persuasive manner fails to win them over, she can wrestle and subdue even the orneriest of the bunch.

Kelsey, a young girl in her early twenties, works as Dorothy's assistant. No two persons could be more unalike than Kelsey and her boss. She is a small, petite little thing, barely weighing a hundred pounds. Her mannerisms are also the opposite of Dorothy in that she is most outgoing and talkative. Kelsey is known to have a soft spot in her heart for all types of dogs—from the most regal to the ugliest. She simply loves dogs and knows each of their canine customers by name. It is rumored among the canine owners that she can actually carry on conversations with those four-legged creatures that come to Waggin' Tails for beautification.

Both Dorothy and Kelsey have many stories of unusual incidents that happened at their business. The two of them can enthrall a listener with the enthusiasm with which they relate a recounting of past events at Waggin' Tails. Many of these stories involve both the dogs themselves, and in some instances, their owners.

This is a story about one of those incidents that occurred at Waggin' Tails and involves some of their canine customers. But rather than have Dorothy and Kelsey relate the story, we turn to one of the participants—Fred.

ॐ

You no doubt have seen dogs doing television commercials. They have been the center of attention in dog food commercials, and tag-alongs in beer, medical product, health food, and car commercials. It seems that television viewers can't get enough of seeing someone walking a dog on a leash while a voice talks about the necessity of buying this or that product. But, I'll bet you never heard a story *told* by a dog. Well, this may be a first, because my name's Fred and I'm a dog.

I was born a wiry haired terrier mutt—locality and pedigree unknown. You have probably seen other terriers like me. It seems that our wire hair sticks out in clumps, both on our body and face. Sometimes I have trouble seeing because the hair on my face seems to stick out and curl down over my eyes. No one would ever say that I'm good-looking or handsome, in fact some have called me a mangy mongrel.

A terrier is defined as "a small, active dog bred for hunting animals that live in burrows." Now, it is true that I'm small, and like all other terriers I've met, I am active. Sometimes I get in trouble for my "activity," and this has a part in the story I'm about to tell.

The first thing I can remember is living in an alley with a few other dogs. We all got along pretty well, but there were times when I had a disagreement with another dog. I may not have always won those scuffles, but I never lost one. Then one day, two men with nets on long poles came into the alley and captured me and one of my buddies, a long-legged hound dog. They put us into the back of a truck and hauled us off to the dog pound.

Well, let me tell ya, I sat around in a large caged area with a bunch of other mutts and nothing to do but tell stories among ourselves. We would argue once in a while and I had a few scuffles but nothing to brag about. Then one day some people came to look around, and lo and behold, they took one of the other mutts away. This went on over a period of time, and sometimes one of my cell mates would go off with the people. Then, after many days and nights of living in that caged area and eating the lousy food, it happened to me.

One afternoon I was taking a snooze in the sun when some barking woke me up. Sure enough, some people were walking by our area and looking at all of us. They were pointing and talking and laughing. I think they were laughing at some of us. Then, wouldn't you know it, a woman pointed her finger at me and said, "Oh, isn't he cute. What's his name?"

Of course I didn't have a name, I never did. After some talk between the woman and the pound people, she declared, "I'll take him." From that moment I became a pet. That's how I ended up in the home of Mortimer and Mildred Klackenhammer. She said that I "looked like a Fred," so that became my name.

Let me tell you something about my new owners. They lived in a nice house and I had the run of a small backyard. I was the only dog, but they did have a little yellow bird in a birdcage on the back patio. That bird never shut up. It would cheep-cheep-cheep all day long. You can bet that I sure would've put a stop to that if I ever got the chance.

One thing I learned right after I came to live with Mortimer and Mildred was that she was the boss. She was about a head taller and huskier than her husband. Poor ol' Mort did whatever she ordered him to do, and when she ordered him to do it. He was what one would call a hen-pecked husband. But I couldn't complain—I had it made, two square meals a day and a warm place to sleep. Mildred and Mort would take me out for walks at times. Of course, I had to learn to walk on a leash, but after some spiteful occurrences, I finally gave in. In the long run it was a good thing, I got to walk around the town and saw many other mutts walking on leashes.

It soon turned out that every Monday, Wednesday, and Friday afternoon Mort would take me for one of these walks. This became our regular routine. It seemed he was happy to get out of the house and away from Mildred. He got a big kick out of stopping and letting me lift my leg and mark a spot as we went along our way. These markings would usually be on a fire hydrant or a light pole, but also included trees and hedges. When I did this he would say, "Atta boy, Fred." We got along well, but I really felt sorry for him. It seemed that his only joy in life was getting out of the house to take me on these little walks. So, I decided to try something to cheer him up.

It seems that along our usual walking route there was a small establishment called Pete's Place. Inside they dispensed alcoholic beverages and assorted foods such as pickled eggs, sausage, and peanuts. You might ask how did I know this. Well, we dogs can sniff out such delicacies. So the plan was to get ol' Mort to go inside and enjoy some of the pleasures of Pete's Place. I thought this over and decided that on Wednesday, which was our next walking day, I would try to steer him into Pete's.

Well, Wednesday came and I was determined to put my plan into action. As we walked along and approached Pete's Place, I began to pull on the leash by trotting faster. Ol' Mort wasn't able to hold me back and had no choice but to begin to trot himself. As we got in front of Pete's, I suddenly turned to my right and into the entry. I was able to pull Mort with me right on through the swinging doors and totally inside. We stopped, Mort looked around, and with a smile on his face, said, "Fred, you mangy, wire-haired mutt, it looks like you wanna stop here. And I don't mind if I do." So, we stayed.

Pete's Place turned out to be just what my sniffer told me it was—a small place with a bar, some tables and chairs, a jukebox, and peanut shells on the floor. As it turned out, there was a regular crowd of old duffers who would show up, have a few drinks and tell some lies. Mort ordered a Scotch and water and some pickled eggs. I got to sniff around in the peanut shells to find bits of spilled food. We to fit right in. This place was like heaven to the both of us.

We stayed in Pete's Place for nearly an hour—or time for two Scotch and waters, four pickled eggs and a sausage. It was great fun and Mort left with a smile on his face. As we walked away he said, "Fred old buddy, this just may turn into one of our regular stopping places, this was a great idea you had." I was really proud. As it turned out we did stop there every Monday, Wednesday, and Friday afternoon. We just fit right in and soon became two of the regulars. I noticed an obvious upturn in Mort's personality and he really looked forward to our little excursions. And, I must admit, so did I. Of course, we never told Mildred about our secret watering hole.

So, this was my life with Mortimer and Mildred Klackenhammer before I was introduced to Waggin' Tails. That introduction happened because of Mildred.

One afternoon she invited some of her snooty bridge club friends over for coffee, and of course, she had to show me off to them. I could tell as soon as they saw me it was not going to go well. They were real snobs and just not friendly like the guys down at Pete's Place. None of these highfalutin women dared to pet me or even pat me on the head. They just stood back with their noses in the air. Their comments ranged from, "Eee-yuuu," and "Oh my goodness, what's that?" to "What kind is he?" and "He's a bit on the scruffy side, isn't he?" They sure weren't my type of crowd.

Well, it was this reaction from her friends that gave Mildred the bright idea to have me made more presentable. That's how I ended up going to Waggin' Tails every other Tuesday morning. Mort would take me there and walk around the shopping center until my ordeal was over. Anything to stay away from Mildred.

The first time I went was quite an experience. This woman named Dorothy got me in a strangle-hold and dunked me into a tub of soapy water. Now I'm not unfriendly to water, I even like to be out in the rain—but *this* water had soap in it. Then she took a brush and scrubbed me all over, even the top of my head. Finally she stopped the scrubbing, let the soapy water out of the tub, and rinsed me off with a hose. She then took me out of the tub, stood me on a table, and began to dry me with a large towel. I could have just shook a couple of times and would have been fine, but no, this woman was intent on rubbing every drop of water off me.

That scrubbing was bad enough, but then she really did it. After I was dried off and standing on the table, I got trimmed. That's right, trimmed. That woman actually took scissors and cut my hair. She trimmed the hair on my body, my legs and tail, and even my face and neck. I was humiliated—my personality was totally gone. I wasn't sloppy-looking and scruffy anymore with my wire-hair sticking out all over. I'd be embarrassed to go to Pete's Place.

Well, as I told you, this every other Tuesday thing at Waggin' Tails became the norm. Sometimes Dorothy bathed and trimmed me, other times a girl named Kelsey did. She was nice and I liked her, but my-oh-my could that girl talk. She talked all the time. She never shut up. If she wasn't talking to me she was singing to me. But, we got along just fine.

Then one Tuesday, fate happened. I saw her. An angel was brought into Waggin' Tails for a trim. The purtiest little female mutt I had ever seen. She was just a bit smaller than me, had long, blonde-colored hair, and big black eyes. She was a real looker and I was smitten. It turned out her name was Minnie. Now isn't that a neat name for a good-looking little dog?

You do know that us dogs talk with each other, just like you people do. We have many ways to talk. We can bark or snarl or whine. We use our tails to point straight up, droop down, or plain ol' wag. We can use our ears to raise up, droop down, or just kind of smile. Sometimes we dance around, crouch down, or paw the ground. We can use many ways to get our point across, and I used all of them to tell this little beauty that I thought she was swell. She would bat her eyes at me and smile, and this just knocked me over. What a lady!

But all was not well. There also appeared every other Tuesday my competition—a tall, white dog they called Throckmorton. Can you believe that for a dog's name? This long-legged dandy was shaved to the skin everywhere except for tufts of white hair on his chin, top of his head, each foot, and the end of his tail. He even wore a jeweled collar around his neck. Yes sir, Throckmorton was a real milquetoast. He definitely would *not* fit in at Pete's Place.

You know how someone or something just rubs you the wrong way? Well, this is the way Throckmorton rubbed me. I did not take a liking to this perfumed foo-foo that was supposed to be a dog. And to make matters worse, he got eyes for my new-found lady friend, little Minnie. By coincidence all three of us happened to end up at Waggin' Tails every other Tuesday morning for our grooming appointments.

Now, for this story to make sense you have to understand the arrangement inside Waggin' Tails. When you walk in the front door there's a waiting room with some chairs, a couple of small tables with lamps on them, and several magazines scattered about. The back wall of this waiting room has a door that opens into the grooming area.

Also on this back wall is a large opening which allows you to see into the grooming area from the waiting room.

Inside the grooming area there is a desk up against this wall with the opening. Dog owners stand in the waiting room to make payments or schedule appointments with Dorothy while she is seated at the desk. There are several small, one-dog cages where the customers are placed while they wait their turn to be groomed. There are two tubs for washing and two tables for drying and grooming. Both Dorothy and Kelsey can work on dogs at the same time. When dogs arrive they're put into a separate cage until their time to be groomed. Then Dorothy and Kelsey take them from the cage and proceed with the bathing and grooming.

It just so happened that this one Tuesday we all three were at Waggin' Tails at the very same time, sitting in cages, waiting our turn. It was at this time that Throckmorton made some smart remark about me, and I answered him back. Well, this little argument went on for a while until Dorothy took me out of the cage and began to give me a bath. Kelsey took Throckmorton out to do the same. This ended up putting us both on tables, side by side. The remarks continued between us and were getting pretty heated. You see, we just didn't like each other. He thought I was an unsophisticated cur, not good enough for his crowd, and I thought he was a bona fide sissy with those tufts of white hair on his chin, head, feet, and tail.

We had just finished being groomed when both Mort and Throckmorton's owner came into the waiting room. She walked up to the opening where the desk was located, and wouldn't you know it, she turned out to be one of those snobs that Mildred had over for bridge that day when I was "introduced." In fact, as I remember, she was the one who suggested I be taken to Waggin' Tails for grooming.

The rest happened so fast I can hardly remember. Dorothy set me on the floor and went to the desk to wait on Throckmorton's owner. Kelsey had just placed Throckmorton on the floor and was retrieving his collar. That's when he made another remark I didn't like and I went after him.

Now, when you've gone through life as a little dog, you learn that when you're in a scuffle against a big dog, you have to go low. So I did. In this type of situation, low-man wins. We both started to stand up on our back legs and sort of lunge into each other as dogs do when they scuffle. But then, to get low, I suddenly ducked my head, burrowed under this unsuspecting dandy, and grabbed him on the inside of his back leg. I bit down hard and we rolled over a couple of times. His owner, standing at the opening, could see our scuffle. She gasped and began to scream, "Stop, stop! Let him go, you monster! Somebody help my baby!" Mort just stood there watching with a smile on his face.

Throckmorton was able to break loose and I went after him and the chase was on. Someone had opened the door between the waiting room and grooming area and we ran through it. The chase went around the waiting room, back into the grooming area where we made a circle around the grooming tables, and back out to the waiting room. We knocked over a table and lamp, scattered magazines, jumped into and over the chairs, and generally created quite a scene. All this time I was right on Throckmorton's tail—in fact, at one point I grabbed hold of the end of his tail and bit off the tuft of white hair.

When all the dust cleared, I was being held in big Dorothy's arms, she had tackled me as I ran past her. Throckmorton was being held and hugged and talked to in baby-talk by his hysterical owner. He was panting, had a bloody bite mark on his back leg, and no tuft of white hair on his tail. Ol' Mort was smiling, patted me on the head and whispered, "Atta boy, Fred."

It turned out that Throckmorton's owner changed his grooming appointment from Tuesday to Thursday so he wouldn't have to be here at the same time as "that uncivilized heathen." This meant me, little ol' Fred.

Well, to top off this story, the next day was Wednesday, and as usual, we stopped at Pete's Place. Mort had a great time telling all the guys about the scuffle. As he told it, "Ol' Fred not only whipped that sissy, but took the snowball off the end of his tail." All the guys came over and said things like, "Atta boy, Fred," "Good going, Fred," "Get this ol' boy a sausage." It was a great day and I was real proud.

Pets and More
The Ant Farm

By Gloria Getman

Gloria Getman

Most days are fairly predictable. The sun comes up, bills arrive in the mail, the neighbor's dog barks too much. Things like that. People go along thinking they have life pretty well figured out.

And that's why Doris Catzberg expected the box she was about to open would contain exactly what she'd ordered for her customer.

Doris was the owner of Pets & More, a pet store situated in the North Point Mall. She'd been in business two years, and it'd been a good experience, so far. She'd managed to keep a variety of cute kittens and puppies available for sale. The parrot, Feathers, she'd named him, was from Costa Rica and very popular with the children. Fish and fish tanks were a steady seller, along with pet toys, leashes and grooming products. She was pleased with what she'd accomplished.

Occasionally, one of her customers would ask her to order something special. Like Mark Hansen, who wanted an ant farm for his eight-year-old son. It had been easy to find a supplier. She'd simply located a site online and placed the order.

Now, as she examined the carton, she noted that it had been stamped "Fragile" and "This Side Up." It had taken nearly three weeks for the order to arrive, and she was anxious to find out the condition of the ants. She'd expected the package to be around 20 by 20 inches, maybe a little larger due to packing material. But this box was three times that size. When the delivery truck had arrived, the driver had loaded it onto a cart with a hydraulic lift to bring it in and place it on her work table.

Doris got a utility knife from under the counter and carefully sliced the wrapping tape on top. As she was about to pull back one of the flaps, the chime at the front of the store indicated a customer had entered. She set aside the knife and turned her attention to the man who had come in.

"I hope my order has arrived," Mark Hanson said. He was a young father, about twenty-five, she guessed, who worked at the cheese factory in a nearby town. He'd explained that his son was handicapped due to a birth defect and was unable to participate in sports. He thought the ant farm would fascinate his son and make an interesting hobby for him.

"It has," she said. "You've timed it just right. I was about to open the box."

Hanson walked back to the work table where the big cardboard container sat. Doris pulled open the top of the box, lifted out packing material, and they both peered inside.

What they saw was the wooden top of a clear glass case,

but it was a lot bigger than either of them expected.

Momentarily taken aback, Doris said, "I can't lift this out by myself."

"Why not just cut the front corners of the box," he said, "and we can slide it out."

"Sure. Why didn't I think of that?"

As soon as she had the front panel loosened, she removed more thick packing material to reveal the contents.

Doris' eyes bugged and Mark Hanson's jaw dropped. This was no ordinary ant farm. Two huge ants stood on top of a mixture of earth and sand that filled the lower half of the 20 by 30 inch container.

"Good Lord," Hanson said. "Those aren't the kind of ants I was expecting."

Doris blinked. "I ... I don't know what to say."

The ants stood a little over an inch tall and four inches in length, much bigger than the carpenter ants she'd seen when she lived in the northeast. Their antennae flicked back and forth above beady black eyes.

They look almost sinister, Doris thought.

"I'm sorry, Mrs. Catzberg, but I can't take this home to my son. These creatures must have come from a jungle in South America. I wanted a simple kid's ant farm."

"I'll send them back and order from another supplier."

"It's too late. His birthday is Friday. I'll just have to find a substitute gift." Shaking his head, Hanson headed for the front exit.

"Good gracious. What am *I* going to do with them?" Doris pulled the remaining packing from around the case and looked for a packing slip, but there was none. She stood there almost a minute, staring at the insects and wondering who would buy such a display from her store. Maybe a zoo, she thought. She was considering how the heavy container could be moved without causing damage, when her thoughts were interrupted.

"Whatcha got there, Mrs. C?"

It was the voice of Andy Krunkle, a sixteen-year-old high school student she'd hired to help out with clean-up after school. Andy had entered the back door of the building without her notice. He was a lanky kid, who stood six inches taller than Doris, had a mop of black hair, part of which flopped over one eye, and a gold earring in his left ear. A tattoo of a snake slithered out from under the left sleeve of his t-shirt.

He walked up and stood next to her. "Whoa! Those are some ants, Mrs. C. I never seen any ants that size. Where'd they come from, Africa?"

"I don't know where they originated. I ordered a simple ant farm, and this is what arrived. The customer has refused to take delivery. Now I'm not sure what to do with them."

"Boy, wait till I tell the guys at school about these suckers. They won't believe it. They'll all want to come see 'um."

"Now, Andy, you know how I feel about kids wandering around the store unsupervised."

"I'm gonna tell Mr. Bungleson, the biology teacher." Andy didn't seem to be listening. He bent over to get a closer look. "I know he'd be interested in seeing somethin' like them. Maybe he could get the school to buy 'um from you. *That* would be a trip."

Just then the sandy soil in one corner began to move. A tiny volcano of sand erupted and the head of another ant appeared.

Andy straightened with a jerk. "Whoa! Will ya look at that? There's more."

Doris' eyes reflected a mixture of surprise and consternation as the third ant pushed its way into full view. She felt her heart palpitate. "How many could there be under all that dirt?"

Andy scratched his head. "By the size of it, there could be dozens. I wonder what they eat."

"Good question." Doris ran two fingers across her forehead. "Clearly, the supplier neglected to provide any nourishment for them during shipping."

Andy raised his eyebrows and looked at Doris. "Maybe they did, but them crawlers ate it all."

"Could be. Ordinary ants like fruit. I'll get some ripe fruit."

"Hey, want me to go to the store for ya?"

"Good idea. I'll give you some money." Doris went to her desk drawer for her purse and gave Andy a ten-dollar bill. Knowing a boy like Andy was always hungry, she added five more and told him to buy a snack for himself.

A grin lit up Andy's face. "Gee, thanks." He headed for the back door, but paused before going out. "Hey, if you stick that display out by the front window, they'll draw lots of lookers. Might bring in some customers. I'll bet the newspaper would come and take pictures."

❧

By the time Andy returned with the fruit he'd purchased, it was time for him to go home. His mother would be expecting him. Doris turned her attention to the ants, pried up the lid of the enclosure and poured in the entire bag of peaches, plums and mangoes, then stepped back. The ant's antennae excitedly flicked back and forth before they quickly began to devour the fruit.

"The poor things must have been hungry," she remarked as she watched them haul small pieces down the little volcano hole.

Satisfied that the ants were taken care of, she made one last round in the store, checking that the kittens and puppies had food and water, covering Feathers, and putting out the trash. Then she turned the closed sign around on the front door and sighed. She'd deal with the problem of the ant farm tomorrow.

At eight o'clock the next morning, Doris entered through the back door of Pets & More, put her purse and sack lunch away before busying herself with her usual routine of feeding the fish, checking on the snakes and refreshing the water and food for the kittens & pups. Her last stop was the ant farm.

Every bit of the fruit she'd given them the day before was gone. "My goodness. You guys have quite an appetite."

The ants moved close to the glass, their antennae flicking back and forth as if trying to communicate.

"Are you still hungry? I don't have any more fruit. And I can't leave the shop right now."

She put her hand on her hip. "I guess I'll have to share

my lunch." With a frown, Doris started toward the break room at the back of the building. "I hope you like peanut butter and jelly," she called back over her shoulder. "Good grief! Look at me, talking to ants. Maybe I need a vacation."

A couple of minutes later, after dropping her sandwich into the ant's home, Doris went about the work of the day, waiting on customers, dusting and restocking shelves, and placing orders for a few new items. As she worked, she rearranged a couple of displays in order to free up a table to move to the window at the front of the store. She'd decided Andy's suggestion of using the ants to draw customers was a good idea.

When noon arrived, she locked up and walked down the mall to a café. A quick lunch would leave time for a side trip to the fruit stand down the street. Those ants are going to eat me out of house and home, she thought. I wonder if they'd like dry cat food. I have plenty of that.

Later, while returning to the store, she found herself smiling. She'd made the farmer very happy when she asked him for his over-ripe fruit. He'd grinned like it was Christmas and cheerfully filled her grocery bag to the top.

As soon as she let herself in the door, she lost no time making her way to the ant farm. What she saw there almost caused her to drop the bag. The surface of the dirt in the enclosure was alive with ants. They were moving in and out of the little volcano, and across the enclosure to a pile of brown and white particles. Evidently, they were cleaning out their subterranean nest.

She settled on the stool behind the work table, her thoughts in a spin. Could this be all of them, she wondered, or were there even more? She bit her lower lip. There was one thing she knew for sure. It was the nature of ant colonies to grow. How would she manage a larger population—the space, the expense? She stood. A simple transaction had turned into a huge problem for her.

Well, no matter what, she couldn't let them starve. Too much money was already invested. She deposited a generous amount of soft apricots and peaches in the opposite corner from their trash heap, then set the bag on the floor. "I need a cup of tea," she muttered to herself.

But she didn't get very far with that idea. The chime at the storefront sounded and she turned in that direction. A tall, slender man had entered. He was dressed in what Doris thought of as office attire, dark slacks, short-sleeved white shirt and tie. His brown hair was a tad shaggy like he'd neglected a haircut, and bushy eyebrows above blue eyes made him look a bit stern.

As soon as he saw Doris, he said, "Where are they? I must see them." He strode toward her. "When Andy Krunkle told me you have some gigantic ants here, I didn't believe him. But he was so adamant, I had to come and see for myself." He stretched his neck, glancing around the store. "Where are they?"

"Ah, well, yes. Come this way." Doris led him back to where the ant farm sat on her work table.

"I'm Bill Bungleson," he said as he followed her. "I teach biology at the high school." As he approached the display his bushy eyebrows bounced like they might pop off his brow. "By golly, I've read about such insects, but have never seen any live ones in my travels." He leaned over and stared for a moment, then straightened and moved slowly around the enclosure to view the ants from different angles.

After a moment, he said, "Mrs. Catzberg, what you have here is a very rare species, endangered, I imagine. They are Zycopian ants from a remote area in Africa. I have to tell you, it's probably unlawful to import them."

She felt her pulse quicken and her stomach turn sour. If he were right, the result could be serious. She found herself chewing on a fingernail as she watched him leave her shop.

Despite the threat, that afternoon, Doris, with Andy's help, set up the display in the front window of the store. It did attract attention, and a number of people came inside, not only to get a better look at the phenomenon, but to buy supplies for their pets. Her opinion of the ants was beginning to brighten a bit, even though keeping them supplied with food was a chore. She even tried them out on dry cat food. They made short work of it.

The following Monday a letter from the EPA arrived indicating that it had been reported to that office that she was harboring an endangered species in her store. Inspector Harold Nusepacker from the EPA's Northern District would arrive on Friday to validate the report.

Doris' nerves jangled. She was sure she was breaking out in a rash. Those confounded ants were not only going to be the ruination of her business, but were going to put her in jail too. This new threat was overwhelming. What to do? What *could* she do? People had seen them. She couldn't just flush them down the toilet. Besides, she couldn't bear the thought of handling them. They might bite.

Later that afternoon, Doris noticed a dark-skinned man with close-cropped gray hair and a neatly trimmed beard standing in front of the window. He was smiling. A minute later, he entered the store and approached the display.

Doris walked over to him. "May I help you?"

"I pray you will," he said in a very cultured deep voice. "I would be grateful if you would sell your ant display to me."

Thinking about the official from the EPA, Doris wondered what the penalty for selling an endangered species would be.

The man reached in his back pants pocket and pulled out his wallet. "I'll give you three hundred dollars."

"I'm not sure I dare sell them. You see ..."

"I must have them," he said with a tinge of urgency in his tone.

Fearing it was against the law to sell them, Doris was torn. On the other hand, if there was no sign of them in her store when the man from the EPA arrived, she could deny she ever had any such creatures. Stalling for time to think, she asked, "Why are they so important?"

"My wife and I are from a tiny village in north Africa. We immigrated here twenty years ago for my job at the university. One of the things we miss so much from our home country is a special dish we haven't had since we were children—sumquasun. It requires a particular ingredient that's no longer available."

Not making any connection, Doris asked, "What sort of special ingredient?"

"It's called cobula, derived from the finely ground

exoskeleton of Zycopian ants, the ones you have here." He took five one hundred-dollar bills out of his wallet and held them out to her.

"Please," he said with tears in his eyes. "Our fortieth anniversary is Saturday. I have a surprise party planned for her. It would be the most precious gift I could give my wife. You see, she's just been diagnosed ..." He choked on the words.

Doris took the money from his hand and smiled up at him. "Saturday, you say? What time is dinner?"

Traci's Trunk: Gently Used Clothing and Accessories

By Irene Morse

Lisa looked up from the sweater she was folding and saw him. He was standing at the cash register, talking with Susan. He was pointing to something in the display case.

Oh, my gosh, thought Lisa. That's the jewelry case. Is he buying jewelry? Is it for me? Does he know I'm working today? Can't he tell that I can see him there, looking at the jewelry? You can see everyone in the store. I can't just walk up to him and ask what he's doing.

Trying to look nonchalant, Lisa went back to folding sweaters. Good lord, she thought, why do people think they can just pick up something and toss it back down? Couldn't they at least make a stab at folding it again? Jeez, people!

Lisa wasn't sure why she was feeling grouchy. Her boyfriend...is that what he was, a boyfriend...was buying her jewelry. Sure, he was getting it from the second-hand store where she had an "extra" job, but it was jewelry. After getting off to a shaky start, maybe Steve was trying to make it up to her, maybe this was his way of saying he was sorry. It bothered Lisa a little that she didn't know him well enough to figure out what he was doing or why.

They had known each other only a few weeks. It was about the same time she had come to work at Traci's Trunk – Gently Used Clothing and Accessories. Lisa clearly remembered the day they met. She had walked into his classroom, introduced herself to Steve, and burst into tears.

Lisa was not generally prone to tears, particularly in front of strangers, strangers she was going to ask for a favor, for heaven's sake. She hadn't realized how close to melt-down she was, so she was as surprised as he was when it happened. She took a few minutes to pull herself together, and to wonder how much she should tell him. She was there to ask a favor, but she didn't want to appear pitiful.

Lisa's divorce was new enough to still be painful, new enough that she still sometimes questioned whether she'd made the right decision. When she was feeling confident, she knew that she couldn't raise her son in a household where her husband responded to challenges with his fists. She couldn't bear it if Mark grew up to be that kind of man. When her confidence was low, she wondered if she had all that much to bring to a relationship anyway, and Jimmy did have many good qualities. Lisa's thoughts churned around in her brain in an endless loop.

When Lisa had finally found the courage to leave Jimmy, she had landed a job as a checker at the local Food Mart. She and Mark moved into a tiny apartment close enough that he could walk to school, and much to her own surprise, they were getting by. At least at first.

Then the dentist told her Mark needed braces, and Mark seemed genuinely desperate for cleats for after-school soccer, so she found the part-time job at Traci's Trunk to pay for the extras.

She wasn't worried right away when the school called to tell her that her usually sunny and cooperative son was "acting out." Mark was almost thirteen, isn't that when children were supposed to act out? Hadn't she read that somewhere? When he started being disrespectful, almost threatening, at home as well, Lisa was on the verge of panic. He needs a positive male role model, she thought.

Although he had never hit Mark, Jimmy's violent nature and his treatment of her had provided the boy with a dark picture of a "manly man." Lisa wondered if that was what was causing the changes in Mark's behavior.

She thought often about how to find a better role model for her son. Mark had talked about how much he liked Mr. Foster, his science teacher. He became more interested in science and it was, "Mr. Foster" this, and "Mr. Foster" that.

One morning, while getting Mark off to school, she had an idea. She would meet with Mr. Foster and see if he would be willing to ... to what? To take Mark under his wing? To pay a little additional attention to Mark? How much could she ask this overworked public-school teacher to do? Well, it was her Mark, this was important, and she had to try. Perhaps Mr. Foster could be the role model she had hoped Jimmy would be for the boy.

So that day she had waited outside the door when class let out. She had dressed carefully, had rehearsed what she should say. She had not prepared for that unexpected and embarrassing gush of water-works.

Having finally pulled herself together and apologized about a dozen times for her childish behavior, she finally got around to stuttering out why she was there, what her son needed, what she was asking of this geeky-looking science teacher. She told him that she realized that she was asking too much, but she just didn't know what else to do. She told him that they didn't have much, but she would find some money somehow to pay him if he would agree.

Mr. Foster leaned forward, and much to Lisa's surprise, put his hand on her knee.

"So, you're willing to pay me to mentor your son?" he asked.

"Yes," she replied, gulping it out in a small voice.

"But you don't have much money, you say?"

"No, but I have an extra part-time job. I could ask for more hours."

"What if I don't want money? What else would you be willing to pay?"

Frightened and desperate, Lisa jumped to her feet. And demanded, "What are you talking about?"

"I think you know," he had replied with a smile. He scribbled something on a piece of paper and held it out to her. "Come to my house this evening at seven and we'll talk some more about terms."

I won't go, of course, Lisa said to herself all the way home. Who does he think he is? What a jerk, and he's not even that good-looking. When she could stop fuming, she wondered if maybe she had misunderstood.

He's a popular science teacher, well-respected, she

thought. Or is he? Mark thinks he hung the moon, but Mark is almost a teen-ager and doesn't always make good decisions. Still, a teacher wouldn't do something like that, would he? He's a teacher.

By the time dinner was finished and Mark was bent over his homework, Lisa had convinced herself that she must have misunderstood what Mr. Foster was proposing. She was feeling kind of sheepish, and wondered if there was some work Mr. Foster needed—help with recording grades, or something. Surely, he was just being nice because he realized they didn't have much money.

Lisa kissed the top of Mark's head and, told him he could watch TV as soon as his homework was done. She told him she had an errand to run, she'd be home in about an hour, and was out the door.

She rang the bell and stood by the front door looking around. Nice neighborhood, she thought.

Mr. Foster opened the door, said "come in," and turned and walked away.

"Do you want a glass of wine?" he asked.

"Sure. Thanks." Lisa replied. She didn't want a glass of wine, but she wanted to be polite. She perched on the edge of a chair in the living room and waited for him to return.

He handed her a glass of wine and kept one for himself. "Mark's a good kid," he told her. "Why does he need a mentor?"

"He's been having problems at school lately, and I thought he might be working through some things about the divorce."

"So, you're divorced."

"Yes, pretty recently." Why did her voice keep getting smaller? What was she afraid of—or worse, ashamed of?

"Okay, come on." He took her hand and pulled her to her feet. He led her down a hallway and into a bedroom. She looked around at the sparse furnishings, the bare walls, the unmade bed.

"I'll see what I can do with Mark. Take off your clothes."

"I. I don't want this." Lisa stuttered.

"Then why did you come?" he challenged. "You knew what this was about. And, besides, do you want help with your kid, or not?"

Lisa was suddenly filled with shame. Why had she come? How had she convinced herself that this isn't exactly what he was proposing? She swallowed hard, sat down on the edge of the bed, and thought, maybe it won't be too bad. Maybe he'll be good for Mark, and this will just be a bad memory.

As she began to undress, Lisa thought that Jimmy had been right. She was nothing but cheap trash. No one worth very much was going to want her for anything but this. Lisa knew that she wasn't beautiful, and she wasn't very smart. What did she have going for her? She didn't even know that a teacher could treat a person this way.

She unhooked her bra, turned to face Mr. Foster—she still thought of him as Mr. Foster—and said to herself, this is for Mark. This is all for Mark. It will be worth it soon.

Lisa walked into her apartment a little before nine o'clock. Mr. Foster had not taken long, and had moved into the living room with another glass of wine by the time Lisa was dressed. He held the glass up as a kind of toast and said, "I'll call you," so she knew she was meant to just leave.

She was so numb by the encounter that she didn't even think about anything but getting home and taking a shower. She turned on the car radio, but she wasn't really hearing it. Somehow, she made it through the evening until Mark was safely in his bed before she threw herself down and wept uncontrollably. Eventually, she fell into an exhausted sleep.

Steve—Lisa thought of him as Steve now—called her sporadically, maybe a couple of times one week then not again for a couple of weeks. He never tried to make small talk, just told her what time to be at his house. She always went.

More times than she could remember, she promised herself she wouldn't go. It didn't seem to her like he was spending any extra time with Mark. She had carefully asked Mark about "Mr. Foster" a couple of times, but he had shrugged it off. "It's fine, Mom. School's fine."

Sometimes, when she was with Steve, she almost thought she was with Jimmy. Jimmy hadn't bothered very much with how she felt either, and he made it pretty clear he didn't have any respect for her. Jimmy was good at pointing out her faults, at demanding his needs be met whether those needs were meatloaf for dinner, or for sex.

"You're my wife," he would shout, "you cannot say 'no.' It's not legal for you to deny me." Then he would either hit her with his doubled-up fist, or have sex with her—sometimes both.

Lisa had never heard that a man could rape his wife. She just tried not to think too much about anything when Jimmy was like that. She also tried not to think too much about anything when Steve was demanding her payment for mentoring Mark. She always hurried home, though, and cried silently in the shower.

"Are you trying to rub the buttons right off that sweater, girl?"

Lisa jumped like she'd been shot as Susan's voice reached through her thoughts. "Oh, my gosh," she gasped, "I didn't hear you walk up. I thought you were with a customer."

"The nerdy guy?" Susan asked. "Yeah, he bought that zircon pendant we got in last week. Funny the things people buy, and funnier still the things people give away. I thought for a minute he might buy that fur with the fox heads and tails to go with it. They're about the same era."

"Yeah," Lisa nodded and formed a weak smile.

"Listen, girl, I'm going to go grab a sandwich for lunch. Will you be okay here by yourself?"

"Sure, it's not very busy today anyway."

Lisa watched Susan walk out of the shop in her fashionable pumps, a scarf thrown carelessly over the shoulder of her turquoise silk blouse. I so badly want to be you, Susan, Lisa thought. You would never find yourself in the predicament I'm in.

Lisa had recognized Susan right away when she applied for the part-time job at Traci's Trunk. Susan had been a year ahead of her at John Muir High School, and Lisa had adored her even then. Susan had been thin, but with a nice figure. Her skin was that milky white that some red-heads have. Her hair was thick, slightly curly, and a magnificent red-gold color. Susan was always on the honor role, president of her senior class, and dating the cutest boy in school.

Susan had not recognized Lisa.

"Uhm, do you do the hiring for Traci?" Lisa had asked shyly at the interview.

"Oh, there's no Traci, girl. Well, that is, I guess I'm Traci," Susan had replied with a laugh.

Lisa thought Susan had the most beautiful laugh, and was on the brink of reminding her that they had gone to the same school. There was something that was pushing into Lisa's memory though. Something about some gossip that had been mean. Something about Susan leaving school suddenly and not being heard from again. Something about that cutest boy in school dating one of the girls on the cheerleading squad.

Well, Lisa was thinking now, it couldn't have been all that bad, just look at her today. Business owner, single but not seeming to care, active in the community, respected.

Lisa was glad that Susan had interrupted her sour thoughts about Steve. She finished out her shift at Traci's feeling up-beat and looking forward to the dinner she had planned for that night. She was fixing fried chicken and French fries, Mark's favorites.

When she got home and noticed the answering machine blinking, Lisa almost didn't listen to the message. She didn't want anything to spoil the evening she had planned to spend with her son. She was hoping Mark might give her a clue into any special relationship he was forming with "Mr. Foster." It broke her heart that Mark was struggling in life, and she hoped the special dinner would let him know how much she loved him.

Still, it might be important, she thought and pushed the

"play" button on the machine. When Lisa heard Steve's voice, her heart sank, but instead of setting up a meeting at his house that night, he was asking if she would join him for lunch on Saturday.

Oh, gosh, she thought. First he's buying jewelry and next he's taking me to lunch. Maybe this thing can work out for everyone after all. Lisa called Melanie and made plans for them to switch shifts at the Food Mart so she could have Saturday off.

During dinner, she asked Mark if he would like to spend Saturday with his friend, Robby. He jumped at the chance, and Lisa smiled, knowing her son would much rather spend a day with his best friend than with his mother. After they ate, Lisa called and made the arrangements with Mary Jane. MJ, as she preferred, was a single mom, too, and they sometimes traded kids when one of them had to be gone.

Now, what will I wear? she mused.

Saturday was bright and sunny. Lisa hummed softly as she dressed carefully, and even added a little mascara to her eyelashes. She grabbed twenty dollars from the envelope which she added to each payday to make payments on Mark's braces. She was going to need to put gas in the car. The place Steve was meeting her for lunch was an hour's drive, but with a beautiful mountain view. Lisa was disappointed, but not surprised, that Steve wasn't going to pick her up and drive her to lunch.

She parked her own car, rather than using the valet parking at the Mountain View Restaurant, and stepped inside. Her eyes were still adjusting to the darkened room when a rather tall man wearing black pants and a white jacket asked if she was meeting someone.

"Yes," she replied with a smile. She mentioned Steve's name and followed the man to a table near the windows that offered the magnificent view. Lisa was so enthralled with the restaurant, the view, and the idea of having lunch in this nice place with Steve that it took her a long minute to realize that there were two people already seated at the table.

Confused and disappointed, Lisa sat, shrugged out of her sweater, hung her purse on the back of her chair, and managed a weak smile. While Steve was ordering white wine for all three of them, Lisa took the chance to glance at the young woman seated next to him.

Oh, gosh, she's young, she thought. She can't be more than twenty or so. Maybe it's Steve's daughter. She's very pretty. Even when I was her age, I was never that pretty.

The young woman had the bluest eyes Lisa had ever seen, and long blond hair. She was too thin for her clothes, and Lisa thought she had seen the top she was wearing at Traci's. She had dropped her head slightly, and Lisa thought she looked both shy and as confused as she herself was.

After the wine was delivered, Steve reached over and touched Lisa's arm.

"Lisa, I'd like you to meet my girlfriend, Christie. Christie, this is Lisa."

"What?" Lisa's head snapped up and she looked from Steve to Christie, and back to Steve.

"Christie," Steve replied, pretending he thought Lisa hadn't heard the name. He slipped his arm around the young woman's shoulders and gave her a squeeze.

Christie, whose face was beat red, kept her eyes on the table in front of her.

Girlfriend? thought Lisa. What am I, a potted plant? Oh, my gosh, look how young she is. She's miserable, too. What is this man doing? He must be at least fifteen or twenty years older than she is. Why is he doing this to us?

"Well, are we ready to order?" Steve asked jovially.

Christie moved to pick up her menu, and that's when Lisa saw it. The zircon pendant. Christie was wearing the zircon pendant. He had planned this—all of this. He had shopped in Traci's Trunk on purpose. He had known she'd be at work that day. He had counted on Susan telling her that he had purchased the pendant. Then he had waited, and finally planned this lunch.

Is there any bigger fool in the universe than I am? Lisa wondered. Jimmy was right about me all along. I'm hardly worth the bother. But this poor innocent young girl—for she was just that—merely a girl. What is this cruel man doing to her? What will this do to her?

The anger struck like a physical force. Lisa had to restrain herself from upending the table into Steve's lap. It wasn't so much what he had done to her, all of the shame he had heaped on her—and that she had actually earned—these past few weeks, but this poor girl. Lisa's maternal protective instincts kicked in and she was as angry as she could ever remember being.

How do they know? Lisa wanted to ask someone. How do they know which women they can do this to? In her wildest dreams, she couldn't imagine something like this happening to Susan. Is there something about us that marks us a fair game? Do we walk differently, or talk differently? How do they know?

Lisa mumbled "Excuse me," grabbed her purse, and ran to the restroom. She stumbled into a stall, locked the door, and threw herself down on the stool. She wanted to scream, to cry out, to rip Steve's face off. She wanted to cry and never stop.

She didn't know how much time had passed before she pulled herself together enough to leave the stall. She didn't know what she wanted to do exactly, she only knew she wasn't going back to that table. She hated leaving Christie in Steve's clutches, but she couldn't do anything to help her. Besides, maybe that innocent-looking girl was actually in on the whole thing. Who knew?

Lisa remembered that she'd left her sweater on the back of her chair. Oh, well, she'd replace it with one from Traci's. She was outta there!

She cried all the way home. She cried tears of anger. She cried tears of self-pity. Then she cried tears of anger again. She managed to stop crying long enough to call MJ and ask if Mark could spend the night. By the time he got home the next day, Lisa looked as sick as she told Mark she was.

Sunday, she called Food Mart and told them she had the flu. And then she cried some more. She worried about Christie and she cried about her, too. Mostly, though, she cried over what a ridiculous, shameful fool she had been.

By Monday morning, Lisa didn't have any tears left, she was simply empty. She heard Mark getting ready for school and moved into the kitchen to fix herself a boiling hot cup of coffee. As he passed through the kitchen, Mark grabbed a piece of bread from the toaster and bit off a hunk. He hoisted his backpack onto one shoulder. As he passed by, he kissed Lisa on the cheek and mumbled, "Bye, Mom. Love you."

What just happened? Lisa wondered. Did Mark just say "Love you" to me? When was the last time I've heard him say those words? It had been a while. Lisa felt a small smile tug at her lips even while trying not to read too much into it. "Wow," she whispered," just wow."

Today was Lisa's scheduled day off at Food Mart, but she was due at Traci's at 11 o'clock. Time for one more cup of coffee though, and she let her thoughts drift back to the weekend just past.

Now that the tears were gone, Lisa felt the anger creeping back. Okay, I'm some kind of fool, she thought, but that doesn't give him the right to treat me like a piece of trash. All I did was ask for help with my son. What kind of person does that? I may not be worth much, but I'm worth way more than that miserable bastard. She banged around the house, her thoughts tangled and running in a loop.

As she was rinsing her coffee cup, it suddenly occurred to Lisa that "Mr. Foster" could very well take his anger at her out on Mark. Oh, Lord, she thought in panic, what could he do to Mark?

Nothing. He will do nothing to my son! If he even thinks about it, I'll go to the principal. Lisa couldn't even imagine how she could go about telling someone what had happened. How gullible and cheap she had been. How mean and cruel he had been from the very start. But she would. She had no doubt about that. If Steve tried to mess with Mark, she would take him down.

As soon as she walked in the door of the shop, Susan grabbed her by the shoulders and demanded, "Good grief, girl. What happened to you?"

"I look that bad, huh?" Lisa whispered.

Susan walked to the door of the shop, locked it, and turned the "Open" side of the sign around to "Closed." She ushered Lisa into a chair.

"Okay, spill it," she said kindly. "What in the world is wrong? Is it Mark?"

"No," Lisa began, "it's me. Just stupid, trashy me." As soon as the first words were out of her mouth, and much to her own surprise, Lisa began to pour her heart out to her boss. She didn't spare herself, but she didn't make light of Steve and what he'd done either. She described her shame, and her overwhelming anger. She talked about sweet, probably innocent, Christie.

When she was finished, Lisa sat quietly, her hands folded in her lap. Susan let the silence linger for a while. Finally, she stood and pulled Lisa to her feet. Gently she guided her over to the only dressing room in the shop. Pulling aside the curtain, she stood Lisa in front of the three-way mirrors in the tiny room.

"Well," she asked, "what do you see?"

"See?"

"Yes, what do you see in the mirrors?"

"Well," Lisa responded in a small voice. "I see two women."

Susan carefully pulled herself to one side out of view in the mirrors and asked, "Now what do you see?"

"Uh, a woman. Pudgy."

"What else?"

"Her clothes are cheap. Her hair is dishwater blond. She's not pretty."

"Now I want you to look a little closer. What does this woman look like inside?"

"I don't understand."

"Do you see a woman who buys her clothes at Traci's Trunk so she can buy her son soccer cleats?"

"I guess so."

"Do you think a woman who leaves an abusive marriage is courageous? Do you think a woman who makes a terrible mistake, but vows to never make it again, is wise? Do you think a woman who worries about a young person she doesn't even know is kind? Do you see that woman here?"

"Uh ... "

"Lisa, what three things would you like to see as you look into these mirrors?"

"Well, someone who is strong. Maybe someone who is smart." Lisa's voice trailed off.

"Okay, we'll start with two." Susan gave Lisa a wink. "Now, I want you to come right here, to this dressing room, every day that you come to work here. Pull back the curtain, look into these mirrors, stand up straight, and state in a firm voice, 'I am strong and smart.' Understand?"

"Why are you doing this?" Lisa asked. "Why do you care how I feel?"

"Well, for starters, I like you Lisa. You do whatever it takes for you and your son. You have a nice sense of humor, and you are kind. You treat everyone who comes in here the same, whether it's someone donating her daughters thousand dollar, used once, prom dress, or someone with a passel of kids in tow trying to find them some pants for school."

"Well, I ... " Lisa's voice trailed off. She tried again, "But, but, you're ... Susan."

"Yeah, I guess I am," came the reply with a giggle. Don't think for one moment that I haven't needed someone to give me a little boost. I had a really bad time my senior year in high school, got into some major trouble. Someone helped me to see that I was separate from my trouble, bigger than it was. I'm just paying it forward, and I expect you will, too, when the time comes. And it will come, Lisa.

"Also, I need you. You buy your clothes here, but you have a knack for putting together outfits. I saw you help that lady who needed something professional-looking for a job interview. I'll bet she got that job, she looked like she'd been shopping at Macy's. You're good for Traci's Trunk, Lisa."

All Lisa could offer was a quiet "Mmm," as Susan walked away to unlock the door for a waiting customer. She glanced once more at the three mirrors and wondered what Susan saw in there that she didn't.

Lisa didn't hear from Steve, and after a while she quit jumping when the phone rang. She stopped hesitating to listen to the messages on her answering machine, and on back-to-school night, she skipped the science class.

One morning, a few weeks later, Susan came into the shop and noticed Lisa standing in front of the dressing room mirrors. She heard a firm voice state, "strong" and "smart." Then she watched Lisa walk resolutely over to the sweater table, shake her head, and with a sigh, begin re-folding sweaters.

Velma June's Discount Coffin Shop

By R. L. Boling

It all started when Uncle Eustis went to meet his maker.

Aunt May Bell, the family matriarch, usually took care of these things, but she was tied up with her youngest daughter's divorce. It seemed that her son-in-law of twenty-plus years had discovered he preferred men over women. Then there was her granddaughter's wedding plans, which had to happen in a hurry, or at least before the first baby shower.

So, Aunt May Bell handed off Uncle Eustis' internment to Velma June. This was her first exposure to the funeral business.

Uncle Eustis was one of those nice old men who had been around the family forever. Velma June wasn't even sure how or if he was related to her. He'd just always been there.

He was invited to all the family events: birthdays, graduations, weddings, and they took turns having him to dinner on holidays. He became a resident of Happy Gardens

Retirement Community, shortly after the state revoked his driver's license when he and his '68 Oldsmobile came to rest atop a fire hydrant after demolishing a bus stop. The old boy had had some type of desk job with the county roads department and should have had a decent retirement, but he had not managed his personal finances very well and died with less than two hundred dollars to his name, after all the bills were settled. Velma June was on the hook for the funeral expenses.

During the four AM bed check, it was discovered Eustis had died peacefully in his sleep. Someone called the coroner's office, and then the next of kin, in that order. The coroner collected him later that morning.

May Bell suggested Peterson's funeral home to Velma June, saying she had used them for years. Velma June made an appointment and met with Timothy, the eldest of the three Peterson brothers. She got the grand tour of the facility, before Timothy took her into his office. An hour later, she virtually staggered out of the building. All told, they wanted more than fifteen thousand dollars to consign Eustis to the grave. On the drive home, Velma June decided not only no, but *hell no*.

After dinner that evening, she talked with John, her husband. He also said, "Hell no. Eustis was a good enough guy, but the old fart wasn't worth fifteen thousand dollars on his best day." He took a deep breath. "I've got no problem helping out but there's a limit." When Velma June agreed, he continued, "My cousin, or is he a second cousin, Rolf, is an undertaker down in Patent, just over the county line. Give him a call."

"But what do we do with Eustis?" Velma June asked.

"Where is he now?"

"He's at Peterson Brother's Funeral Home."

"They can hang on to him for a while, I guess."

Velma June called the number John had given her and found out Cousin Rolf had sold the mortuary and retired. When she finally tracked him down, he agreed to meet with her.

After a really nice lunch in a shabby little diner Rolf had picked, he heard Velma June's tale of woe. He snorted and looked at the ceiling a moment before he spoke. "Well, the Peterson boys are scoundrels, and that's a fact."

"But, what am I going to do about Eustis?"

"Well, my mortician's license is still valid, so we can use it."

"I don't understand, why?"

"We can start our own mortuary."

"What will it cost?" she whined.

"Less than the Peterson boys will charge. Hell, we'll open our own shop. We might even turn a profit. We are going to need a building, and a cold box. I've got everything else in storage." He looked at his watch. "You find us a building and give me a call. I'm late for my golf game."

"Why are you doing this?" she asked as he stood.

"Two reasons: One, you're family and I like your husband. Two, I can't wait to hear the wails of protest from the Peterson boys." He chuckled and walked off.

That night Velma June didn't have a chance to talk to John before he left on a business trip. Two days later, she related her conversation with Rolf. John sat, thinking for a long time.

Finally she asked, "What should I do?"

John's response startled her. He laughed, slapped his knee and said, "You better find a building to rent."

Velma June remembered seeing a FOR RENT sign on one of the vacant stores at North Point Mall and went there to check if it was still available. She was in the process of writing down the phone number printed on the sign in the window when a young man approached her. "May I help you ma'am?" he asked politely.

"I'm starting a business," she said, "and this seems like a good location."

"I'm the property manager. Would you like to take a look inside?"

"Yes, please."

After Velma June signed the lease, she went for the second item on Rolf's list, a cold box. Rolf was on a fishing trip in Baja, so Velma June called Jim Fisk, the coroner, to ask for advice. She had gone to high school with Jim, and he owed her, big time, for the junior prom fiasco, anyway.

Jim gave her contact information for the two companies he knew that had that sort of equipment. The bids she received for the stainless steel monsters both companies said would meet her needs cost more than her house.

When Rolf returned, she presented him with the bids. He smiled. "Those are nice, but not necessary."

He called a restaurant supply house and ordered a cold box for less than a tenth of the lowest bid.

"But, those are for food, not people," Velma June complained.

"Dead vegetables, dead people, cold is cold. The dead don't care," he quipped.

When Rolf inspected the building, he brought along a tape measure and two rolls of two-inch blue painter's tape. With Velma June holding one end of the tape, he measured and marked locations for walls, doors, the cold box, and an office. Their business began to take shape – on the floor.

Once he was satisfied, they packed up. As they were getting ready to leave, Rolf took her over to the back corner. "This is where the cold box goes, door here." He pointed. "If I'm not here, make sure they set it up just the way I have it marked." He indicated the square of blue tape on the floor with a big "X" through it.

"Okay." Velma June replied. "Who's going to build the walls? Do we need a contractor for that?"

"No, not really, I'll have the lumber and drywall delivered and find some day laborers for the walls. We will need to find an electrician though. I'll take care of that later."

Velma June liked the idea of being in business and having a real job. After college her only job had been wife and mother.

The first day at the shop, she brought a card table and two chairs and set them in the taped-off area of the future office. The second day she brought a book and a portable radio.

Two days later, a truck loaded with building materials showed up at the back door of the shop. The deliverymen unloaded everything onto the parking lot, and informed her they weren't going to put it inside. She told them to take it back. The men put the building materials inside, Velma June signed for them, and called Rolf.

"Good, they're early. See you tomorrow." He hung up.

Velma June was amazed how rapidly the construction progressed. One of the workers, Juan Sandoval, became the foreman by default, being the only one who spoke English well enough to communicate with Velma June.

All the laborers worked for cash. At first, she had been nervous about carrying all that money in her purse. But, there were no problems. At the end of each day, she sat at her card table and made sure each worker was paid what he was owed.

With the framing finished to Rolf's satisfaction, the electrician came and ran wires, hung lights, and installed outlets and switches.

Juan was called back to hang the drywall. He brought his nephew, Poncho, to help. On the last day of sanding the drywall joints, before painting, Juan's teenage niece, Dorothea, came to clean up. She diligently swept floors, washed windows, wiped down the walls, and did an exceptional job of cleaning. Velma June was so impressed that she hired the girl to clean the shop and Velma June's home.

The next day, Rolf brought the paint. By six that evening, Juan and Poncho had every interior wall painted.

On his own, Rolf had gone down to City Hall to obtain their business license. In the space on the form that asked for the business name Rolf got whimsical. He boldly printed "Velma June's Discount Coffin Shop." Thus the Coffin Shop was born.

As they locked up that night, Velma June invited Rolf

home to have dinner with the family. During supper they discussed the things they had to do to open.

"First we need a coffin for Eustis," Rolf said between bites.

"Where do we buy one?" Velma June asked.

"Buy is expensive, how about make?"

"Dad's got his wood shop," John Junior volunteered.

"Your father has a job, and you don't know what you're talking about," his mother said.

"Wait a minute, Velma June," Rolf said, "Let's hear what the lad has to say."

John Junior smiled. "Well, Dad's got that new CNC router thing. I'll bet we could turn out a coffin with that."

"Hmm," Rolf stopped eating. "How would we go about that?"

ॐ

After the meal was finished, they adjourned to John Junior's room and his computer. Using the software that came with the CNC machine, they designed a coffin that made the best use of two plywood sheets.

When Rolf and Velma June were satisfied with the design, they went to John Senior's shop and created several scale models. They settled on a simple keyhole coffin.

Rolf showed up at the house the next day with six sheets of three-quarter inch furniture grade oak plywood strapped to the top of his Toyota. The first two attempts didn't turn out well and were discarded. The third try turned out a perfect keyhole coffin.

Velma June convinced John to allow the Coffin Shop to

borrow his CNC router, and it was relocated to North Point Mall.

Juan was called back. The wooden coffin was sanded and given two coats of Varathane.

Rolf and Velma June were admiring the finished coffin as it dried atop two sawhorses in the back of the shop when Rolf suddenly exclaimed, "Oh shit. I forgot the hearse."

"Hearse?" Velma June asked. "You mean one of those over-sized Cadillac station wagons? So, what's that going to cost?"

Rolf took out his phone, "Don't know. Let's check Craig's List."

"You can get a hearse on Craig's List?"

Rolf chuckled, "Probably, but all we need is a van." He continued fiddling with his phone. "Ah, here we go. A 2003 white Chevy van, no body damage, $3,200, and it's local."

He called the number in the advertisement and the following afternoon Velma June drove the company van— she just couldn't call it a hearse—over to Signs by Stan. Stan called two days later to say it was ready.

Rolf and Velma June drove over to pick up the van. The only words Velma June could find to describe the graphics on the side of the van was tacky, very tacky.

Velma June was a firm believer in insurance, lots of insurance. The company van was, if anything, over insured. "I hope someone does steal it, we could make some money," Rolf commented.

That Friday night they parked the van behind the Coffin Shop. Monday morning it was gone. The police found it three day later. It had been the centerpiece of a party—what the police called a rave—out in the county on a ditch bank. Every usable part had been removed and what was left had been burned. The insurance company wrote the business a check for $7,500. Velma June hadn't mentioned Rolf's comment.

The replacement van was a slightly newer, nicer, powder blue Ford, with a less tacky sign.

❧

They picked up Eustis from Peterson's, who had been threatening to charge rent for keeping him, and brought him to the Coffin Shop. Velma June wouldn't allow Eustis to be buried naked. She found a nice suit at Tracy's Trunk. She took one of her husband's shirts and a tie he didn't like. John Junior donated a pair of shoes and socks.

❧

In what Velma June thought of as a sign of the coming apocalypse, or her grandmother's impending dementia, the old woman had purchased twenty acres of Valley Glenn Memorial Park when the cemetery had fallen on hard times in the 1960s. Velma June selected a plot for Eustis under an old and majestic oak.

On a sunny day with dandelion clouds on the distant hills, Eustis was laid to rest. Rolf's contribution was the head stone—a two foot by three foot slab of snowy marble. Deeply etched into the stone, in two inch letters, were four lines:

Cpl. Eustis W. Page USA
1921-2019
Beloved Uncle and Friend
Rest in Peace

The family was surprised to learn Eustis was Episcopalian. Father Simon, from Happy Gardens, presided over the graveside service. There were ten mourners in attendance: John Senior, Velma June, Patty, John Junior, Rolf and five of Eustis' friends from Happy Gardens Retirement Community.

After the grave was closed, the family retired to Peabody's Steak House for lunch and drinks. Patty drove home, with John Junior in the front passenger seat, giggling about the condition of the adults. Rolf spent the night in the guest room.

∽

The adults sat around the breakfast table, drank coffee and ignored Patty as she happily made breakfast.

"Well, what now?" John asked. "I mean now that we've got old Eustis all tucked away."

Velma June sipped at her coffee, "I don't know."

Rolf lifted his head off his folded hands. "I do." He smiled. "We keep the business going."

"Why?" John asked.

"Well, we provide a service..."

"But at what cost?"

"Okay, Velma June doesn't need a salary. I don't need a pay check. All the business has to do is cover its own expenses."

"He's right, John. We've spent all the big money. Besides," Velma June smacked her fist on the table as she finished, "I want to."

John sighed. "Really? You want to deal with dead bodies?"

"Well, no. The bodies are creepy, but I like helping people."

"I'll help with the bodies," Patty said from the kitchen, "I mean, they don't bother me."

Her mother and father stared at her.

"I helped Cousin Rolf dress Uncle Eustis."

"Did she?" Velma June asked.

"Yes, she did. She even trimmed up his hair."

"Did you really?" John asked in amazement.

"When I was little, and the older kids picked on me, I'd climb up into Uncle Eustis' lap. He protected me. I liked him."

Rolf looked thoughtfully at Patty, "None of my offspring wanted anything to do with my mortuary," he mused. "You get your license, kid, and my half of the Coffin Shop is yours."

"Deal." Patty grinned and flipped another pancake on the griddle.

ও

A week later Velma June was sitting in the office of the Coffin Shop when the little bell over the front door tinkled. She walked into the big room, "Hello, may I help you?"

An older couple stood close together by the door, the man removed his hat. "Yes ma'am. We come to see about gettin' our boy, Bobby, buried."

"Please, come in," Velma June led them into the office, "I'm so sorry about your son. What happened?"

The woman took a tissue from her purse and dabbed at her eyes. The man cleared his throat. "Bobby was hang-in' around with some bad people and... Well he got his-self killed by the police."

"I'm so sorry. Where did this happen?"

"Out in the county, west of town."

"Have the authorities released his body?"

"I don't know, ma'am." He hesitated, "Ma'am, the problem is...we don't got a lot of money. See, we went to the other fellows, the ones with that big fancy building on the other side of town."

"I know who you mean." Velma June frowned. "Where is Bobby now?"

The mother began to cry. Her husband touched her arm. "We don't know."

"Let me make a call." Velma June picked up the phone and dialed the coroner's office. "Hello. Jim Fisk, please."

The couple did not hear the response.

"Tell him Velma June would like word with him, please." There was another pause, "Jim, this is Velma June. Do you have a young man by the name of Bobby?" She looked at the father, her eyebrows raised in question.

"Fisher, ma'am. Robert Fisher."

Velma June smiled at them. "Robert Fisher."

There was another pause. "Really? Why?" She listened to the explanation. "Well make it a priority. Mr. and Mrs. Fisher are here in my office, and they want to bury their son." She hung up the phone a little harder than was necessary. "Oh that man." She sighed.

She turned to the couple. "I'm sorry. The coroner says it

will be a couple of days before he can release the bod... your son."

"But, ma'am..." Mr. Fisher began.

"Yes, cost. We don't do fancy, we offer a plain wooden coffin. No silk lining, no frills. We start at $500."

Mr. Fisher nodded.

"Have you arranged for a burial plot?" Velma June asked.

❧

Patty began working at the Coffin Shop when she turned seventeen, and was soon transporting the deceased. There were times when she would ferry their guests, as Velma June called the deceased, to cemeteries and other mortuaries in and around their city. Patty came to call her transport services "Uber for the Dead."

The current van, a puce 2006 Dodge, had a working radio and cassette tape player. Always concerned about the comfort of the dearly departed, Patty played classical music during the trip to their next physical destination. She played Wagner for Mr. and Mrs. Peabody—an elderly couple who had died in a car accident.

She delivered the Peabodys to a funeral home in an adjoining county. She was on her way home, singing along with Pink, when she crossed the city limits and became aware of the odor of burning motor oil. The check engine light came on and the motor began making odd sounds. Looking in the rearview mirror, she saw smoke wafting behind the van.

After pulling onto the shoulder of the road, she removed

the key, grabbed her purse, quickly jumped out and moved to the front of the van, away from the now billowing smoke. She was in the process of taking out her phone when flames began licking the windshield. She pressed 9-1-1, explained the situation, and gave her location.

Five minutes later, a city police car pulled up, and Officer Jack Simon strode around the burning vehicle.

"How many vans have you lost this month?" he asked. "Is this number three or four?"

"Actually, this one is the current record holder. We've had it all of four months," she quipped.

"Ah, there's no body in there, is there?" Jack posed the question hesitantly.

"No, just me." Patty's gaze never left the vehicle, the flames growing larger, and now curling around the bottom.

"Let's move across the street before this thing explodes." He placed a hand on her back and guided her to the sidewalk as the fire truck arrived, followed by the wreaker.

The fire was quickly extinguished and the charred hulk winched onto the carrier.

Watching the two trucks slip into traffic, Jack turned to Patty. "Now what?"

"I called my mother, my father, and my brother, but no one answered." She shrugged, and adjusted her purse strap.

He punched his thumb over his shoulder. "There's a nice little diner about a quarter mile down the road. Would you like a cup of coffee?"

"Sure. Can we add a slice of pie? I haven't eaten all day." As they moved toward the patrol car, she wrinkled her nose and added, "I don't have to sit in the back, do I?"

"Not unless you want to." He smiled and opened the front passenger door.

❧

As time went by, word got around that Velma June's Discount Coffin Shop was providing dignified and reasonably priced funeral services. The business grew, and was actually quite profitable.

Early one morning, just after Velma June had unlocked the front door, two plain clothes city police officers came to the Coffin Shop. She had known the older of the two officers, Sergeant Thomas Decker, since high school. The other officer was introduced as Jack Simon. They begged her to donate her services for a young woman who had been the unintended victim of a drive-by gang shooting. She had no family and no money, they explained. The officers thought the young woman deserved something better than what the county could provide, cremation with her ashes placed in a plastic bag and dumped in a wooden box made in the prison workshop, and burial in Potter's Field in a vertical plot with the cremains of five other people.

❧

Velma June's actions endeared her to the less fortunate of the area. The down side of her altruism was that it cost her more than money.

Early one morning she was awakened by a call from Office Simon, insisting that she come down to the mall. She arrived to find a young child, in a position of peaceful repose, lying atop the doormat at her front door. The body was surrounded by fresh cut flowers. Two large candles glowed softly in the predawn darkness.

Though not Catholic, Velma June crossed herself and said a prayer for the child as tears ran down her cheeks.

The coroner took the body away. As the crime lab technicians loaded the flowers, candles, and Velma June's doormat into their van, Officer Simon showed Velma June the note that had been left with the child. She held the translucent evidence bag up to the light from the sign in the window of the Doughnut Hole. The words, written on a soiled scrap of notebook paper, tugged at her heart.

THIS RAOUL HE GOOD BOY
PLEASE BURY HIM WITH HONOR
HAVE PRIEST DO SERVICE PLEASE

It looked as though it had been written with a felt marker. The lettering was crude and something she couldn't read had been crossed out at the top of the page. There were several spots that might have been tears.

The coroner released the body twelve days later, after the cause of death had been determined. The report said Raoul had died of natural causes, complications of pneumonia. Patty, Velma June's daughter, took the coroner's call and told him she would be over as soon as she could.

The child's body, found at the Discount Coffin Shop, made the local news, and even got some play on a late night radio talk show. Someone started collecting donations and another concerned citizen set up a GoFundMe account.

Fifty mourners were at the cemetery to witness little Raoul being laid to rest. Velma June hoped the boy's parents were among them.

When the third body was discovered at the Coffin Shop's front door, the chief of police asked Velma June to install security cameras.

The donations were another matter. A local radio talk show host talked about the total amount of money that had been raised. To head off any repercussions, and with the help of her lawyer, Velma June established a nonprofit to provide funerals for the community's indigent. With Monsignor Rodriguez and the chief of police on the board of directors, no one questioned where and how the money was spent.

They had started Velma June's Discount Coffin Shop using Uncle Rolf's funeral director license, but he was getting on in years and wanted to retire—again.

Velma June had gotten her own license, but she had a real problem handling the bodies.

On the day Patty turned eighteen, she became a full-time employee of the Coffin Shop. She graduated from high school three months later, and enrolled at the community college. Rolf saw to Patty's training. She had no problem with the deceased. She had a little ritual of formally introducing herself to the late Mr. or Ms. Dead and proceeded to carry on a very one-sided conversation.

As Patty's knowledge of the funeral business increased, and she came closer to obtaining her associate's degree, and then her funeral director license, Rolf left the day-to-day running of the business to Velma June and her daughter.

Rolf passed away five years after making good on his promise to give Patty his half ownership of Velma June's Discount Coffin Shop. Patty took care of Cousin Rolf's preparations. It was the first time Velma June had seen her daughter cry since she was ten years old.

The Coffin Shop broke several of their rules. Rolf was laid to rest in a plain wooden coffin. But, it was lined with white silk satin and his head rested upon a pillow of the same fabric.

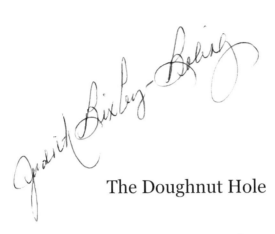

The Doughnut Hole

By Judith Bixby Boling

May Lynn Church listened to the news on NPR as she drove her Mercedes through the deserted pre-dawn streets. She would arrive at North Point Mall precisely at five fifteen, park in her space behind The Doughnut Hole, and be inside as Jimmy Doland finished baking the confections to be sold to the morning commuters after the shop opened at six.

She confidently turned right from Minor Street into the wide alley behind the strip mall. Out of habit rather than need, she pushed down the turn indicator lever, negotiated the corner around the back of the shops, palmed the steering wheel to slip into her parking stall—and stomped on the brake. Her body lurched forward, the seatbelt pulling taut across her chest. Her mouth hung open in disbelief.

Stacked in *her* parking stall—the one with her name stenciled on the pavement in twelve-inch letters with white reflective paint—was a pallet holding fifty sheets of furniture-grade plywood.

"No. No. No," May Lynn shouted, and slammed her fists on the steering wheel before opening the car door, and getting out.

She saw Juan Sandoval and his nephew, Poncho, climbing into their 1972 Ford pickup.

Working through the night, when the stores were closed, the men used the plywood to build coffins in the back room of Velma June's Discount Coffin Shop, a low cost, no frills mortuary—next door to May Lynn's establishment.

May Lynn started toward the truck, pointed at the parking stall and shouted, "Move the plywood. Before you leave."

Juan nodded his head while flashing a toothy smile. "I'm moving my truck right now, Mrs. Church."

"NO." She shook her head violently. Her thick, shoulder-length black hair flew in both directions, slapping each cheek alternately. "That wood is in my parking space."

"Sorry, Mrs. Church. We're going home just now. We'll move the wood when we come back tonight."

She stomped her foot, and marched closer to the truck. "But, it's in my parking space. You have to move that wood."

Juan slammed the door, turned over the engine and backed the truck into the alley. The vehicle stopped. May Lynn involuntarily cringed when she heard the gears grind as he threw it into first. The engine roared, and the tires squealed. The truck sped towards Major Street.

Her shoulders slumped when Juan turned onto the thoroughfare. She retraced her steps, backed up the car, and parked in the space next to the plywood.

As she exited her SUV, she thought she saw movement in

the shadows where Juan's truck had stood. *It's probably some homeless person who spent the night back here,* she thought, and moved to the back door of The Doughnut Hole.

The screen door bounced off the back wall, and slammed against the door jamb as the spring snapped it closed. She gave the door a heavy push, allowing it to slam shut. She walked past the lavatory and through the store room to her office. After flipping on the lights, and dropping her purse and keys on the desk, she made her way to the front of the shop, still fuming and muttering curses.

"What's up, Mrs. Church?" Jackie Stewart asked, while sliding a tray of apple fritters into the display case.

"Let me know when Velma June comes in. There's plywood in my parking space."

"Again?" the girl asked, turning to take a tray of maple bars from the rack.

May Lynn poured coffee into her favorite mug, and returned to her office. Sitting behind her desk, she sipped the steaming hot brew, and turned on the computer. Out of the corner of her eye, she thought she saw someone pass the open door, and called, "Good morning, Jimmy." May Lynn shivered. *The air must have cycled on.*

There was no response. She shrugged. *He must be heading to the little room.* She turned her attention to her unread email.

☙

A half-hour later, Jimmy Doland appeared at the doorway. "Good morning, Mrs. C. I made the extra crème-filled and jellies like you asked."

"Thanks, Jimmy. Have Jackie box them for Mrs. Epstein. She'll pick them up this afternoon." She clicked on an email from Mary's Shoe Mart.

"Already spoke with Jackie. She has the order form. I'm going home. See you in the morning." He took a step back, then pivoted to go out the back door.

"Bye," May Lynn said absentmindedly as she tried to decide whether to order the one-inch black pumps with peep-toes, or the emerald green sling-backs with four-inch heels. She shrugged and ordered them both, as well as a pair of red ballet flats.

❧

At fifteen minutes to eight, Jackie saw Velma June's Cadillac slip into the parking space next to an older lime green van. "Lady, I'm sure glad I'm not you today," she said, watching the well-dressed woman exit the sedan and pull out her cell phone while staring at the door of the Coffin Shop. Jackie sprinted to the back to alert May Lynn.

The bell over the door tinkled. Jackie put on her "doughnut shop" smile. "Good morning, Miss Velma. What can I get you this morning?" The girl was already at the coffee pot, filling a large paper cup.

"Just coffee this morning. Some generous person left a little something on my doormat. The police and coroner should be here in about ten minutes." Velma June frowned at the éclairs. "Damn, I really wanted one of those this morning," she muttered, while she dropped several coins on the counter next to the cash register and turned to leave.

"Thank you, Miss Velma. Can you wait a sec? Mrs. C

wants a word."

The woman didn't reply as she stood at the window, staring into the parking lot, and sipping her coffee.

"They put your plywood in my space. *Again*," announced May Lynn as she came around the display cases.

"That's the least of my problems this morning," Velma June said, maintaining her vigil. "Someone left a gift at my front door."

"Bodies are left on your doorstep at least once a month. You ought to be used to it by now. Just get your wood moved, and tell Lowe's they can't be leaving it in my space."

"Yes'm."

A police cruiser came into the parking lot, and stopped perpendicularly to the parking stalls—in front of The Doughnut Hole.

Velma June gave May Lynn a withering look. "Soon as the coroner carts off my unwanted guest." She stepped around the doughnut shop proprietor to go outside and talk with the officer.

May Lynn stared at the Coffin Shop owner, then moved around the display case and picked up a napkin. As she pondered her selection she noticed a young man standing across from her, studying the mounds of doughnut holes, all rolled in a variety of toppings. She didn't recall seeing him when she came out, and decided it was because she had been so focused on Velma June.

After glancing right and left, she said, "Jackie will be with you in a moment."

She placed five chocolate doughnut holes on a napkin and popped the sixth into her mouth. As she moved away, she noticed her finger pads were beginning to wrinkle. *I wonder whether the air conditioning is working properly.* She returned to her office.

તે

Around eleven thirty, May Lynn was northbound on Major Street, returning from the bank after depositing the previous day's receipts. As she prepared to turn left to park behind the shop, she saw the brown UPS truck blocking the alley. She continued to the intersection. Negotiating the left turn onto Minor Street, she noticed the police and coroner were still in the parking lot. *Well, that's not good.* She made another left into the alley, and waited for a pair of older women, one bent nearly double and using a cane, going in the back door of The Pot Spot.

She parked in the space she'd recently vacated, grabbed the strap on her purse, and glanced over the hood of her car as she got out. The young man she'd seen earlier in the shop was sitting atop the plywood, his back to her. May Lynn started to speak to him, but changed her mind and went inside. Sitting at her desk, she pondered the man outside. *Why is he hanging around?*

She stood abruptly, went to the front, waited while Jackie finished serving a customer, then asked, "Did you see the young man in front of the case this morning? He was looking at the trays of doughnut holes when Velma June went outside."

Jackie sighed. "I would have helped him if I had. What did he look like?"

The proprietor thought a moment, trying to picture him.

She opened her mouth, but closed it again. "Never mind," she murmured and walked away, shaking her head.

"The woman is losing the few marbles she has left," Jackie muttered.

May Lynn strolled down the hall, still trying to formulate a description. *I've seen him twice. What does he look like?* She couldn't recall his features. *What is it he wants?* Her gaze was trained on the floor as she returned to the office. *Goodness, it's cold in here.* She rubbed her arms, felt gooseflesh and retraced her steps into the hall to check the thermostat. It was set at seventy-two degrees.

Back in the office, she looked up the number for the air conditioning repairman. With her finger poised over the keypad, she was stunned to see the young man sitting in the upholstered chair across from her.

May Lynn scrutinized him. He looked to be in his late teens or early twenties. Dirty blond hair hung over his forehead and into his eyes. His faded plaid shirt was covered in blood, as were his worn jeans.

May Lynn dropped the receiver into the cradle, leaned against the chair back, and muttered, "Oh crap. Not another one. Are they all coming from the Coffin Shop?"

"Am I dead?" he asked.

"I believe you are." She pushed herself upright. "Do you remember what happened to you?"

He looked thoughtful and spoke slowly. "Me and Jenny Lynd were at the old Ashford Drive-in. At first we just talked, but then I kissed her, and we started makin' out." He squirmed.

May Lynn flinched as she watched his hand passed

through the thick arm of the chair. "Go on," she instructed.

"Well, I got her blouse unbuttoned, and..." his voice trailed off again. "You know." He looked away.

Can ghosts blush?

She nodded, tilted back her head, closed her eyes, and sighed loudly. "You're George Chesterfield."

"How did you know that?"

"You and Jenny Lynd have been missing for three weeks. It was assumed you ran off to be together. Pictures of you both have been all over the news." May Lynn let George absorb this information. "How did you get here?"

"I don't know. We were at the drive-in. He came, and then we were in a field. There was dry alfalfa stubble. It shoulda hurt to lay on it, but it didn't. I never could figure out exactly where we were. Then, last night, I was suddenly here."

"Is Jenny here, too?"

"I haven't seen her. Not for a while."

"Did she go through the door?"

"What door? What does it look like?" He turned his head, obviously looking for something. "I haven't seen a door or a light or anything. I think he took Jenny someplace else."

"Who did this, George?"

"Mr. Lynd." His voice was nearly a whisper. "Jenny's father. He had an ax."

Abruptly, May Lynn stood. "Stay here," she instructed as she rushed out, and was out on the sidewalk just as the police cruiser and coroner van were leaving the parking lot. "Damn."

She twisted her body as she began to turn toward the

doughnut shop, but faced forward again when something moving in the back of the coroner's vehicle caught her attention. May Lynn squinted, straining to see through the tinted glass in the back window.

A sudden realization came to her. George was waving at her. *It was his body left on Velma June's doorstep.* Hesitantly, she raised her hand and returned the wave. The vehicle moved into traffic on Minor Street. She sent up a prayer for the souls of George and Jenny as she returned to her office to call Crime Stoppers.

Around one o'clock, May Lynn walked down to The Green Burrito for lunch. An hour later, she returned to The Doughnut Hole in a much better mood, owing to the three margaritas that washed down the chili verde and warm flour tortillas.

Stepping inside the doughnut shop, she greeted Peggy Short and Mrs. Epstein. May Lynn hummed a tune she'd heard on the Muzak during her mid-day meal, but stopped, and leaned against the door jamb to her office when she saw the white-haired woman in a brightly colored muumuu admiring the painting on the wall in her office.

"Oh no," she uttered, covering her face with her right hand. "Not another one."

The Palette Store
A Perfect Date

by Shirley A. Blair Keller

Masaki Yukamura was a gentleman and a creative person who lost himself in his work, but the shock of his wife of 40 years walking off with her high school sweetheart, woke him up. He'd ignored her for years, working sunup to sundown, and this was the price. She left, and probably had no idea how much he loved her. What a mistake, a loss, and a hurt he could barely stand. Now what?

He continued his habit of waking in the dark, dressing, drinking a cup of coffee and heading out to the orchards. But now, there was no hot meal waiting at 8:00 when he returned for breakfast, no lunch prepared in the pail to be taken with him so he could work the day through, and no hot supper at sun down when he returned to shower and eat. \

For the first time in all those years, he put himself in her shoes. The loneliness she must have felt almost drowned him. He gasped. How could he have been so thoughtless? The pain cut through like a knife. Now what?

When he returned to the dark cold house, he turned on the kitchen light. In a flash of memory, he saw his childhood at this same table, his mother at the stove preparing breakfast, his father at the head of the table waiting for his meal to be served to him. Masaki realized he'd repeated what he knew. His dad, too, left in the dark, returned to a warm breakfast served by his mom. He saw the boy with a pen in his hand, making drawings on an artist's sketchpad. He'd forgotten how much he loved creating on paper, the dreams he'd had as a child, hoping beyond hope that he would not end up like his father. And yet, that is what he had done with his life, sunup to sundown work. And he had not done a drawing in all these years. As he walked upstairs to his bedroom he vowed to find an art store.

Kate Stanley pulled at the ponytail of her long brown hair, glanced at the mirror behind her desk to check how she looked, and smiled. She then walked down the aisles one by one, checking to see if everything was in place. The store opened in ten minutes. Every morning Kate took this walk, breathing in the smell of the art store. The odor of paints and fine art paper filled the air. This was her dream come true. She'd come to art late in life, after being widowed, discovering that black ink pens with composition journals were cheap forms of entertainment. She woke each morning, grabbed a cup of coffee, and wrote in the wee hours until it was time to dress for work. Writing led to playing with other art forms.

She named the store The Palette Store, and had a shape of a palette carved out of wood, with turquoise lettering hanging above the shop door. The palette had splotches of colors of a rainbow, a paint brush stuck in the red splotch. This store came out of her writing. A dream emerged. Instead of working for others, why not find a way to work at a job she could love? Providing art supplies for customers who were also exploring their creative selves seemed a perfect fit. Kate received a loan from a local bank to add to her savings, and with the help of an investor, here she was, taking her morning walk to make sure everything's in place. She shook her head in amazement.

The only thing missing in Kate's life was a partner. She missed her husband, a soul mate, and a person she loved with all her being. But in all the hard work and time it took to make the dream of the store come true, she had no time to think about how in the world she'd meet anyone to even consider as a partner. Dating was not on her radar. In her free time she played with clay, her favorite creations being masks of various kinds. She painted dots on recycled items, which took hours of concentration. She did not feel lonely. But she knew life was more complete with someone to share it with.

What about placing a personal ad in the local newspaper? Kate thought. Make an experiment out of it. She knew two sets of couples that met that way, and did end up falling in love and marrying. Why not try it? *If it didn't work,* she thought, *I'd still have the store and my studio to play in.*

Kate grabbed a local paper on her way home from work. She poured a glass of merlot, sat down at the kitchen table, and began to read the ads. She skimmed the instructions on how to place ads, and designed her own.

"Seeking soul mate to share life's passionate journey. Gentleman's race is not important. Widowed, 51, non smoking, enjoys writing, art, travel, family, friends, and walking."

It was suggested to leave a voice mail message at an 800 number the ad was connected to, so Kate wrote one, practiced and then posted her message.

"Thank you for responding. My name is Kate. How would you feel about a fishing trip, camping in the mountains, long drives to the beach, back rubs, movies? How about close family and friends gatherings that include mixed races and cultures? And what about curling up with a good book or cooking a good meal and staying home with a video? If you cook that is a plus. I like doing dishes. Do you like theatre, art, music? I enjoy writing, and hope to publish a book someday. Leave your name and number so we can continue this conversation. I'd love to hear your thoughts. Take care."

There was nothing to do now but wait for responses.

For a week, Kate called the 800 number each evening. She was beginning to think this a futile exercise, when on the seventh day there was a message for her.

"Hello. My name is Masaki Yukamura. I am responding to your personal ad. My phone number is 555-1212. Your ad intrigued me. I would very much like to have a phone conversation with you. If you call around 8:00 PM I will be here. I look forward to talking with you." The message ended.

He sounded nice. His name indicated he might be Japanese. He hooked Kate with the compliment about her ad. It was getting close to 7:00 PM.

Should I call him tonight? She thought, feeling nervous, but her curiosity was too great. There was no question, she would call.

The phone rang. She'd written his name on a piece of paper and said it in her head.

"Hello," a man answered.

"Hello. Is this Masaki Yukamura? My name is Kate Stanley. I am returning the message from the personal ad."

"Oh, yes," he said. "I was hoping you'd call tonight."

"Well, I didn't want to wait. You know a little about me, but I know nothing about you. Tell me about yourself?"

"That seems fair," he said, and sounded like he was smiling. Kate relaxed a bit.

"I am of Japanese ancestry, 62 years old. My hair was once dark brown but now streaked with gray. I am five foot ten, 170 pounds, I have a degree in engineering from UCB. I have a farm. I am in the middle of a divorce. My wife left me for a high school sweetheart who showed up at our door not long ago. I have three grown children, the youngest I am helping through college. The divorce is my fault. I worked too much and she felt neglected. And there is something else you need to know. My friends were very worried about me because I was so depressed about the divorce. They introduced me to a woman who lives about a block from my house. She is Mexican, and a lovely person. We have been on a couple of dates, but are not committed. Because she knows my friends, and lives so close, I tend to think we will continue. I am surprised I felt the need to respond to your ad, but I wanted to know who you are. There was something so open about the ad. But, if you do not want to continue, I understand."

"Thank you for telling me about your neighbor. I value honesty. I would not interfere if you have a commitment. That is a line I will not cross. I am interested in getting to know more about you, so if you really have not talked with her about a future, I'd like to continue our conversation."

"Yes, we have been on two dates. There was no conversation about a future. As I said, only because of the familiarity of friends and neighbors, I am considering her. I am curious about you, so here I am."

Masaki related he was Buddhist, health conscious, and eats on the edge of macrobiotics. He has 40 acres of vineyards and fruit trees. They are dividing up the property apart of the divorce settlement. She moved to San Francisco with her new man. Kate was impressed by how easily he told his story. He asked Kate to describe herself.

"I am 5 foot 4, 51 years old, widowed with two grown sons who have families of their own. I am a little overweight, not nearly as conscious of healthy foods as you sound." Kate chuckled, nervously. "I am told I am pretty, with long dark brown hair I wear in a pony tail, that hasn't grayed yet, and brown eyes. I own an art store in North Point Mall, and am an artist myself. I journal every morning," Kate said.

"Being Buddhist, I learned that truth is a basic of life. I appreciate how open you are with your description. Thank you," he added.

The conversation wouldn't wind down. She didn't want him to go. He seemed to feel the same. Fluent in Italian and Spanish, he revealed. He described himself as a quiet soul, not forceful, slow to move these days. He writes things down, and then speaks. He admitted to having a very hard year, which made sense.

Kate said, "You did not choose to have your marriage end, like I did not choose my husband to die. That kind of experience tends to slow people down."

Misaki was worried about Kate's phone bill, but even trying to be considerate, he could not stop asking her questions. He still had to host his daughter for a late dinner that night. She stopped to eat with him every week after her dance class which ended at 8:30.

"I would really like to meet with you. Do you feel the same?" he asked.

"Yes, I would like that," Kate answered.

"How about I stop by your store? I had been planning to shop for some drawing supplies. At the end of your work day we could find some nice place to eat. Would that work for you?"

"That would be wonderful. When would you like to meet?"

"How about Friday evening? I will make a reservation at Bolene's. I'd like it to be a special evening. Is that okay? It's my treat," said Misaki.

Kate bit her lip. This dating process is not like it was when she was younger. Men always paid. But now, women were taking the initiative, and insisted on paying their own way. Makes for no sense of obligation. He was gracious. She felt he would consider it an insult, so she let it go.

❧

On Friday, Kate looked out the window. A white Lincoln Continental pulled in front of the store just after 4:30. *Wow,* she thought. A handsome man, brown hair with gray streaks, glasses, wrinkles around the eyes, walked toward the store. He wore an elegant gray suit. *He doesn't look his 62 years,* she thought. He came through the door, the bell overhead rang. They shook hands in greeting. She didn't want to let go. They introduced themselves, both a little uncomfortable. He gave her a business card. She smiled.

She hoped she looked all right. She'd worn a dress to work, with nylons, jewelry, more formally dressed than is normal for work. Her hair was loose, falling to her shoulders. She was self-conscious because of her weight, but like he said, truth will out, so if it bothers him, then she is not interested in one who is caught up in body beautiful. She'd had enough of that in her life.

"Would you direct me to the drawing supplies?"

"Of course," she responded and pointed to the back of the store, leading him half way, "See, along that wall."

He nodded and she returned to the cash register to close up shop. After he paid, she locked the door while he put his package in the car.

They decided to walk to Main Street. She told him she'd never been to Bolene's.

"You are in for a treat," he said.

They arrived at the restaurant. It was a beautiful place. Stained glass windows, wooden dividers, candle light, white tablecloths, silver set and linen napkins. In the back was a bar, and as people finished dinner the place emptied, and others came to fill the bar seats. Since it was Halloween weekend the waiters and waitresses were costumed as were many of the guests.

Masaki and Kate noticed two carved pumpkins that captured their attention. One was a spider with candlelight flickering through delicately carved webs. The spider seemed so real it could back off the pumpkin and walk away. The other pumpkin was a cat face, done in negative and positive spaces, with delicate lines and extremely feminine. Masaki was fascinated by them.

The waitress arrived at the table, dressed as a black cat, whiskers drawn on her face, little ears on her head, a bow-tie, cute, delicate and very feminine like the pumpkin cat. Misaki asked her if they hired an artist to do the pumpkins.

She laughed, "No. I did them!"

He was thrilled to tell the artist how much he liked the pumpkins. He suggested she take a picture with her head between the two pumpkins. It would be a great picture. And she did it later in the evening before Kate and Misaki left for the night.

"One of the marks of a fine restaurant is, you can have these kinds of experiences with the people who work there," said Misaki. He was really enjoying himself. There was a guitarist playing in the background when they had arrived, and at one point he was replaced with a three piece jazz combo.

Misaki ordered a rack of lamb, explaining he was indulging. This did not quite match the description of his healthy eating habits. Kate smiled, but said nothing. She ordered swordfish with a veggie mix. He had potatoes and she rice. They tasted each other's dishes and raved about the flavors. They ordered coffee and much later he wanted dessert. He ordered a lemon tart and offered to share with Kate. She had one bite and loved it.

The conversation moved easily from topic to topic. He talked about history, religion, asking Kate questions about her religious training, which didn't take long to explain. She had none. She shared her writing process and talked about the various art projects she was playing with. They were both totally engaged. Time seemed to stand still. And the whole time they talked, he sketched on the paper mat that had been put before him. Pumpkins with spiders and cats appeared, one after another, in various poses.

This man is an artist. She was liking him more and more, as each aspect of his personality unfolded. She was beginning to hope he was feeling the same. They were different in some ways, and yet, so compatible. They had no trouble talking and sharing. She knew he was here to explore whether he was making a good choice in his neighbor. She really had no idea what he was deciding about her. She just knew he was enjoying her company, and she his. And rather than worry about the negative, she focused on the present.

His attraction to Kate puzzled him. *Maybe I should take a chance and not take the easy route laid out by my friends.*

જ

At the end of the evening, Misaki gave the waitress the drawing he'd been working on. He and Kate raved about the meal, the music, and how much both enjoyed their conversation. As they walked back to the Mall to get their cars, they agreed, it had been a perfect evening.

"Kate, I think you are a wonderful person. I am torn. I knew there was something very special and different about you when I read the ad. I just had to know what it was. And I am grateful I had this time with you. But, I know me. I work sun-up to sun-down every day. You live just far enough away that it would be hard to make a relationship work. Life will be easier to continue with my neighbor. My family and friends know her and all have expectations. I cannot go against that." He took a deep breath and exhaled slowly. "So I won't be calling again. I hope you know this has nothing to do with you. I am truly sorry."

"It's okay, Misaki. I must say, though, I began to have hope there was a future with us because this has been a most wonderful evening: the food, the music, your artwork, and how easy we are with each other." Kate sighed, and continued, "We are at an age when we know what we can and cannot do. So please do not think about this again. In the moment, it was perfect Misaki, and I thank you. This was a one of a kind evening. Thank you." Kate smiled.

He kissed Kate's cheek, and she held his hand, as their eyes locked for a minute. He reached for his keys, got into the car and backed out of the parking place. She watched him drive off. Kate took a deep breath and as she exhaled, she let him go.

ॐ

The next day was Halloween. Kate did calligraphy on a small thank you card:

Dear Misaki,

Please accept this card as a small token of a large appreciation. Sometimes life's most enjoyable moments are short but sweet. Hope the goblins are kind to you tonight!

With gratitude and warm regards,

Kate

As Kate posted the card to Misaki, she sent along the slightest hope that he might change his mind. He had expressed dismay that he'd followed the pattern of his father, and did not like the result. So, why is he chasing the safest and easiest path? Though her weight didn't seem an issue, maybe she read him wrong and in the end it was a deciding factor in his mind. There was no way to know. So she took him at his word. *Hope Springs Eternal*, she thought, evoking Emerson, and she smiled.

Kate went off to work and sensed that something good was in her future with or without Misaki. There was a short story to finish she'd started the other day. A drawing was developing in her mind. Life was good.

ॐ

The store was humming, people in every aisle. Kate had advertised an end of spring sale in the local paper, encouraging people to stock up with art supplies for the hot summer to come. And it worked. She moved from customer to the cash register to ring up sales. *Maybe I should have found help,* she thought. She worked as fast as she could, apologizing when a line formed and someone looked impatient.

At the end of the day, as she walked through the aisles straightening and jotting down inventory needs on a pad, she was pleased. It had been a very successful day. Exhausted, she longed for a hot shower and bed. She walked to the front of the store to close out the cash register when she noticed a white car pull up in front of her store. Her heart skipped a beat.

It cannot be, she thought.

But there he was, getting out of the car and when he saw her through the window, he smiled. He was dressed casually in jeans and shirt, loafers, and no jacket.

Months had gone by since she wrote the note. She had given up on ever seeing him again. When she remembered the evening and how perfect it was, she shrugged. It was not meant to be.

He opened the door. The bell overhead rang.

"Hello, Kate," he said.

"Hello Misaki, what may I do for you?" she asked.

"I need a drawing pad, and three pens. Am I too late?"

"No, please come on in. You know where it all is."

He walked toward the back a few steps, then turned back to her.

"I was wondering if you have plans for dinner? I would like to talk with you. Only if you are free, of course," he said.

She stared at him. In a split second, she decided to say yes, not to second guess what he wanted, to allow each moment to unfold and see where he is going with this visit.

"Well, I had planned to go to the Green Burrito a few doors down to grab a quick bite before heading home. Would that be okay?" she asked.

"That would be fine," he answered.

"I just have to finish some things here so get what you need," she said.

Misaki turned and walked to the back wall. He picked out a drawing pad, turned to the pen rack and found his favorite fine drawing pens. He returned to the front and handed her money.

She rang up his order, gave him change, bagged the supplies and suggested he sit in the chair by the window. "I won't be long," she said.

He sat watching her do the closing routine.

She felt his eyes on her, as if he was caressing her hair, then face. She was stirred, embarrassed, excited he had appeared, and she tried to stop all expectation of hope building within her. There was no stopping it. He was here and she was happy

They left the store. She turned and locked up. They walked the couple of doors down the mall to the restaurant.

❧

The Green Burrito was Kate's favorite place when she didn't want to make her own dinner. The walls were sponge painted in various shades of green, thus the name of the restaurant. Paintings of different scenes in Mexico graced the walls, all by local artists. Kate's black and white drawing of a bunch of flowers in a vase was included. On her last trip to Oaxaca she'd spent a day in the patio of the B&B, and this drawing was the best one out of the batch. There were dividers between every booth and bouquets of sunflowers were placed against the walls, Kate's favorite flowers.

Kate and Misaki found an empty booth. The waiter placed menus in front of them.

"Good evening Kate, may I get you both something to drink," he asked.

"Hi, Carlos, Yes," Kate answered. "I would like a margarita and water. Misaki, what would you like?"

"That sounds great," he said.

Carlos left.

"I noticed the ad for your sale today in the paper. How did it go?" Masaki asked.

"It went far better than I expected," Kate said. "I was surprised by the response. I should have had help."

"I am happy for you." He smiled.

Kate nodded in appreciation. She decided to wait until he brought up the reason for his visit. She was too nervous to talk.

Carlos delivered the drinks just in time to keep the silence from becoming awkward. And in addition, he had the chips and salsa on the tray. The chips were so fresh you could smell the heat off the tortillas as he walked toward them.

Kate suggested chili verde plates with tortillas, since it was their best meal, checking to see if that was okay. Misaki agreed. Carlos took the order and returned to the kitchen.

They toasted, "Cheers," and each took a sip.

"I suppose you are wondering why I am here," Misaki began.

Kate nodded.

"Thank you for the lovely note," said Misaki. "I do not usually keep thank you notes, but for some reason after reading the note three or four times, I slipped it into my handkerchief drawer. You would think I'd have forgotten it. But I thought about it every day these past months. I am not someone who examines himself much, but I kept asking, if as Kate mentioned in her note, the evening was perfect, memorable, and it even took my breath away, why did I walk away? For convenience? To satisfy friends?"

"I took a look at the situation with the woman I was dating, and not moving the relationship one step further than I had when I met you. What was I thinking? It was very unfair to her." Misaki sighed.

"The answer was very clear, I cannot get you out of my mind. I pulled the note out once every week. I read it over and over. I felt energy flow through me. But I put the note back in the drawer, and continued my life as it was. This morning I took the note out, read it once. I put it down on the dresser, walked down the block to my friend's house, and I apologized to her. We said our goodbyes as a potential couple. I finished my day's work early, and here I am, hoping beyond hope that you want me to pursue you."

Kate sat very still, watching Misaki's face. Carlos returned to the table with two plates of food and set them down. She picked up her fork, then placed it back on the table. She peered at Misaki. He looked so fearful. She smiled. That is how she felt the minute she saw his car pull in front of her store. She wanted this to be the outcome so badly and now that it was, she savored the feeling of excitement, energy flowed through her, just like Misaki described. She wanted to laugh. She knew she must answer him quickly, before he caused himself a heart attack.

"Misaki, I would very much like it if you would pursue me," Kate said, smiling ear-to-ear. "We'd better eat before the food gets cold," and finally she let the laughter spill out.

He smiled, and then, he too found laughter bursting forth in a relief he hadn't felt in a very long time.

Kreate a Koala

By Irene Morse, Elizabeth Morse and McKenzie Morse

"Please. Please. Please, Mom."

Eliza was holding her mother's hand, struggling to keep up with her long strides, and trying to get her attention. They had come to North Point Mall so that Eliza's mom could shop at Traci's Trunk, but they had just passed Kreate a Koala. Eliza had her heart set on doing just that.

"Please, Mom. Pleeeeeaaaaase." Eliza was pouring it on now, her six-year-old voice increasing in volume even as she found an ear-piercing pitch. She stopped walking and looked up at her mother. Eliza allowed a little tear to form in the corner of one eye as she softly begged, "Please, Mommy. Please." Eliza had large eyes, the color of a new-born fawn, topped with thick silky lashes, and she knew how to use them.

"It's okay, Mom, I can go with her," suggested Eliza's big sister, Maggie. "Just pick us up at Kreate a Koala."

Eliza's mom was just about to give in when she heard her

name called. Turning, she saw her friend and co-worker, Jan, approaching from the parking lot.

"Wow, Marilyn," said Jan, a little out of breath, "I didn't think you could hear me with that little siren you have by the hand going off. I wanted to ask you about Phil and Dottie's party." With that, both girls knew that this conversation was going to go on for a while.

"Just pick us up at Kreate a Koala, Mom," Maggie repeated, taking Eliza by the hand.

"Fine," replied their mother absently, handing Eliza some money.

The girls walked into the store hand in hand, but soon Maggie's attention was diverted to a shelf of new arrivals. Eliza moved off a bit and started to shuffle through the animals to find one she wanted to finish putting together. Picking up a handful of unstuffed creatures, and moving a kangaroo to one side, she was surprised to find a baby beneath the pile. A human-like baby that looked like it already had the stuffing put inside.

Whoa, thought Eliza to herself, *this baby looks real.*

Eliza had thought she might want to make a wallaby. She didn't have one of those yet, and it would make a nice addition to her collection. *On the other hand,* she thought, *I don't have a real baby either. I don't even know anyone who does. It could be my little sister. Maggie has me, but I don't have a little sister.*

Eliza went to the accessories section and started looking through the stuff she could add to her baby. *I guess the first thing it needs is a heart,* she thought as she picked one out and wandered back to the shelf to get her baby. She carefully rubbed the heart on her own belly, her cheek, and on her chest. She put it against her forehead for a moment, and then she took the backing off and put the sticker on the baby's chest.

The baby's eyes popped open, it showed a lopsided grin, and spoke aloud, "Well, hello little girl. Are you my mother?"

"Oh! Em! Gee!" cried Eliza. "Maggie, Maggie, come here quick."

Maggie came running. "Are you hurt, Lizey?" she asked. "What's the matter?"

"This baby talked to me, Mags," Eliza stammered.

"Babies can't talk, Eliza," Maggie explained patiently. "They have to be taught."

"This. Baby. Talked."

"Wait. Where did you get a baby? I thought this was Kreate a Koala. Koalas aren't babies, at least not human-looking babies."

"It was right here on the shelf. Under the kangaroo. It was already stuffed."

"I went and got a heart for it," Eliza continued. "I rubbed the heart on my belly, my cheek, and my chest. Then I put it on my forehead for a minute and stuck it on the baby. That's when it opened its eyes and talked to me."

"Seriously, Lizey?" Maggie groaned.

"Heh. Heh. Heh."

"Shh," said Eliza. "Did you hear that?"

"What?" asked Maggie. "I didn't hear anything."

"I think the baby was laughing."

"Lizey, it's a stuffed baby. It can't talk and it can't laugh." Maggie cautiously touched the heart on the baby's chest.

"Hello, little girl. Are you my sister?" asked the baby.

"Holy ... something. This stuffed baby talked, and not in a particularly cute little baby voice. Let's get out of here," cried Maggie grabbing her sister's hand.

"But I'm hungry," whined the baby in a cuter voice, "Won't you feed me?"

"We can't just leave it here, Mags, it's hungry," said Eliza.

"Are you nuts? It's not even a real thing—or if it is, it's a weird thing, and pretty scary."

The baby made a little crying sound, and hiccupped. A tear rolled down its cheek.

"Well, I don't know what makes a baby real," said Eliza, "but this one cries, and talks, and says it's hungry. We need to do something."

Maggie and Eliza stopped talking and gave the baby a good once-over. It had brown hair and pretty blue eyes that were filled with tears at the moment. It had the cutest dimples in its cheeks, and a soft light-tan-colored body with a little round belly. There was something about its lopsided grin that made Maggie uncomfortable, but she couldn't say what it was.

Maggie had lots of pets at home. The truth is, she wanted to be a veterinarian when she grew up. This wasn't so different from her pet hamster, was it?

"Please, Mags, can't we take it home?" pleaded Eliza.

"Mom is never going to let us keep it," said Maggie.

"Come on, girlies, I can help you sneak me past her. Don't you ever do anything your mom doesn't like? Are you just scaredy cats?" sneered the baby.

"I'm not! I'm going to find you some clothes," exclaimed

Eliza and hurried back to the accessories shelf with a clear mission in mind.

"Ya know, Mags," wheedled the baby, "no one else you know has a real baby for a pet. You'd be famous in your school. You might even make a little pocket change showing me off. You'd have to be careful, though, we don't want the grown-ups to find out." The baby narrowed its eyes and flashed a lopsided, mischievous grin.

Eliza returned with her arms filled with clothes. "This is a girl-baby," she told Maggie. "She needs a name."

"How about Sneaky Baby?" asked Maggie.

"No."

"How about Evil Grinning Baby?"

"No, let's call her Mittens. Now help me put these clothes on Mittens, Mags."

The girls dressed the baby. They put a pink and purple polka-dot shirt on her. Then they added some purple leggings and a striped, pink and white skirt. They put tiny pink and white checked Vans on her feet. They added a zebra-striped purse trimmed in pink, because babies have a lot of stuff to carry. Eliza put a jaunty pink beret on her head, and the girls stood back to see how she looked.

"Oh, you are so pretty, Mittens," cried Eliza.

"Heh. Heh. Heh."

"I don't know about this, Lizey," said Maggie. "I don't like that laugh."

"Don't be such a scaredy cat," whispered Mittens.

"No. Mags. Don't be such a scaredy cat," echoed Eliza.

"Now," said Mittens, "you need to make a Teddy Bear for me. It's not that I want a stupid Teddy Bear, but you can put it on top of me when you take me out of the store. Your mom will never notice I'm here."

"And we need a stroller, Mags. Mom won't be able to see what we have in it." Eliza ran off to search for a baby stroller in the accessories department.

"Listen, Mags, you need to get on board with this," snarled Mittens. "You must know that I can do things you haven't even thought about yet. Besides, we're about to have some freakin' good fun. Now, get goin' on that Teddy Bear."

Maggie constructed the Teddy Bear while Eliza went to pay for their creations. She hoped the money Mom had given her to make the Koala would be enough. She put the Teddy on the counter then asked, "How much for a baby?"

"Oh, we don't have any babies here, little girl."

"Oh, yes you do, a girl baby. I made one and I need to pay for it."

"Little girl, we don't have any babies here and I'm very busy. Just pay for the bear, there's a line behind you."

So, Eliza paid for the bear. The sales lady gave her a dollar and a quarter change and asked her to move on.

"Maggie, the lady wouldn't let me pay for the baby. She said they don't have babies in this store. I guess we can just take them both and leave," reported Eliza when she returned. "Maybe I'll just leave the change she gave me here on the shelf."

They put Mittens in the stroller and sat the Teddy Bear on top of her. Then, both girls looking innocent and sweet, wheeled them out the door onto the sidewalk.

Marilyn and Jan were still laughing about who went home with whom from the party. "All done, girls?" asked their mom. She pushed the button on the key fob to unlock the doors to the mini-van. "Go ahead and get in, I'll be right there," she said.

"If they don't have babies at the Kreate a Koala store, Mittens, how did you get there?" asked Eliza as they made their way to the car.

"Oh, some kid brought me over from Chuckie's Toy Store," Mittens replied. "Heh. Heh. Heh."

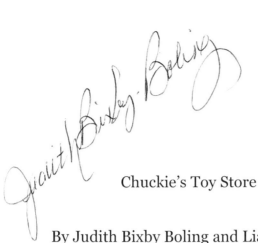

Chuckie's Toy Store

By Judith Bixby Boling and Liam Boling

Charles Baumgartner and his wife, Prunilla, were the first proprietors to rent space in the newly constructed North Point Mall. Extraordinary and unexplainable occurrences were said to take place within the walls of the toy store.

Max Netterfield held the door while a woman and young girl entered the shop. Max and his son, Jack followed on their heels.

"Welcome, come, come to Chuckie's Toy S-S-Store," Vladimir the Mouse stuttered and bent forward with the rush of pneumatic pistons.

Polly and Amanda Morton moved past the four-foot tall robot without hesitation. They were intent on their mission to purchase a birthday gift for Sally Nugent, one of Amanda's friends.

Jack clutched his father's arm, and scrunched his face. "That mouse scares me."

"It's all right, Buddy," Max assured the boy. "He's not going to hurt you. He's just saying hello. Let's see what they have for video game systems."

They strode with purpose to the back wall, which was filled floor to ceiling with games of all sorts.

ॐ

Amanda couldn't resist gazing at the dolls as she followed her mother to the back of the store. She stopped to look at a baby doll lying on the shelf, without any kind of packaging.

The doll was swaddled in a pink blanket. It looked so real. The girl tentatively reached out to touch the doll. Rather than the usual rubber or plastic feel of a baby doll, this one felt like real flesh. Amanda carefully picked up the doll and cradled it.

The girl couldn't take her eyes off the doll. She began swaying from side to side, nurturing it as one would an infant.

"Come along, Mandy, we don't have time to look at dolls today," her mother said impatiently, backtracking to stand beside her daughter. "We have other stores to go to."

"Look, Mama, she's real," Amanda gushed as she held out the doll to show her mother.

"She is very lifelike," Polly admitted as she bent down to get a closer look and found herself touching the baby's cheek. "Oh, my, I wonder how they did that." She knelt next to her daughter, admiring the baby doll.

ॐ

Max was uncertain which game system to buy, and began reading the specifications on the boxes.

Jack shifted his weight from one foot to the other, trying hard to be patient. "Let's get a Nintendo Switch. Bill and Ryan both have Switches. They play games over the Internet."

"I'll take a look at the Switch. I want to see what's out

there. I haven't played video games in a long time," Max said, his finger running down the specs on an X-Box. "I guess they're not making Ataris anymore."

"Yeah, they do, but Atari is lame. Just get the Switch."

Max didn't respond as he returned to reading

Jack wandered over to look at game cartridges. One immediately caught his attention. He picked it up and studied the picture on the box. A man sat on a raft in the middle of the ocean. Debris from an apparent shipwreck floated around the raft. Beyond that was a shark with a human head in its open mouth. A decapitated body floated nearby, the water around it red with blood.

Max glanced over. "Whatcha got there, Bud?"

"This game looks cool, Dad. The guy on the raft has to get all the stuff out of the water before the shark gets him."

Judging the image on the box, Max thought it was a little too gruesome for a nine-year-old, and was reluctant to buy it.

"May I be of some assistance?" Charles Baumgartner asked as he approached the pair.

"My son's interested in this game, but I'm not sure it's appropriate."

"Of course. Would you like to take a look at the game?" Charles took the box from Jack.

"Please, Dad. Please," Jack begged.

"Oh, all right," Max relented.

"Follow me." Charles led them to a room in the back where multiple game systems were set up. After inserting the cartridge into the console, he handed father and son each a controller, and left them to play the game.

≈

"Can we get this doll for Sally? She loves babies," Amanda whined.

Polly wasn't in the mood to argue with her daughter, and thought a baby doll a nice gift. "Of course." She stood erect and proceeded to the checkout counter.

Amanda followed, staring into the baby's face.

"Thanks," the baby said. "I thought I'd never get off that shelf."

The girl stared at the doll, disbelief etched on her face. "Did you talk?"

"Of course. I'm older than I look. So, I'm going to live with Sally? Will I like her?"

"Y...Yes. She's very nice, and loves babies. She'll take very good care of you." Amanda had reached her mother, and gently laid the doll on the counter. "Mama, the baby talked," she whispered.

"That's nice. I didn't see a string. Do you press her hand or tummy to make her talk?" Polly asked as she opened her purse and took out her wallet.

"No, Mama. She really talked."

Polly glanced at the doll, then at her daughter, and to the clerk. "Does this doll talk?"

Prunilla Baumgartner looked at the doll. "I've never heard it utter a syllable. But, then again, I've never been fond of dolls." She pushed buttons on the old-fashioned cash register. "Do you want it gift wrapped?"

Amanda's mouth flew open and color drained from her face. "You can't put her in a box and cover her with paper," she exclaimed, and scooped the doll into her arms.

"Amanda Jane. Manners," her mother scolded, handing

over a credit card. "We'll wrap it at home. Thank you."

After signing the credit card paperwork, Polly and Amanda left the shop, the girl carrying the baby doll.

ॐ

Max and Jack selected their avatars, and started to play the game.

Jack went first, extracting a plastic bag, a piece of driftwood, and a clump of seaweed from the water before the shark allowed the head to fall out of its mouth.

Max pulled out a fishing net, a rowing oar, and a sea chest, which was locked.

The shark started to approach the raft.

Jack sat on the edge of the chair, his feet firmly on the floor. He was able to get a shovel, a glass bottle and a shoe onto the raft.

The shark moved closer.

The boy sat back in the chair and drew up his legs. "Go away, Mr. Shark." You're not wanted here," he muttered.

Max smiled at his son and returned his attention to the game.

The shark was beside the raft.

Most of the debris was further away now, and would be more difficult to retrieve. Leaning over the side would be dangerous—if not fatal. "I wonder how many lives we get in this game," Max muttered, and hauled a small folding chair onto the raft, along with a tea pot and a pair of pants. He checked the location of the shark and decided to try to retrieve a fishing rod.

The shark submerged. It came up under the raft, lifting it

out of the water. All the treasures slid to the edge. The two avatars flailed about as Jack and Max pushed buttons on their controllers, working to keep them out of the water. Max was able to get his avatar to reach up and hook his fingers around the edge of the tilting platform.

The feet of Jack's avatar hung over the edge, his toes in the water. Max made a grab for the other avatar's arms as the character slipped into the sea.

The shark submerged, as well.

The raft lay flat in the calm water.

Father and son stared at the screen, waiting for the return of Jack's avatar. It appeared on the raft with a musical ping. With all the treasure returned to the ocean, they began anew.

A book floated nearby. The word, OPEN, was stamped into the faded and soggy blue cover. The moment Max clicked on the book, an odd tingling came over him.

"Dad," Jack cried, "You're fading."

Max stared at his son. "So are you."

They found themselves sitting on the raft in the middle of an ocean, with no land in sight.

"What the..." Max left the sentence unfinished.

"Are we in the game?" Jack peered over the side into the water.

"It does appear." Max flexed his fingers in front of his face.

The shark had moved some distance from the floating platform and lay in wait.

"Well, this is a game changer. Let's see what's out there that we can use." Max mentally inventoried the floating debris, turning over in his mind how each one might be used to defeat the shark. "If we work together, we can get that rowing oar and the fishing net.

"How, Dad?"

"Well, if I lie on my stomach and reach out, I should be able to catch the net with my fingers. Then, we can use it to guide the oar closer to us."

Jack looked warily at the floating objects and the shark, now circling the raft. "Be careful, Dad."

Max lay on his stomach, his shoulders over the water. With his hand extended, his fingertips just touched the netting. "A little closer," he said softly as he moved his legs and pushed with his toes. His torso hovered over the water, his hips over the edge of the raft.

"Sit on my legs, Jack. I don't want to fall in." He tried to entwine his fingers in the netting.

The boy slowly scooted on his bottom and was lifting himself up when Max said, "Oh, no" and dropped into the sea.

Jack heard the splash and looked up in time to see his father's feet sink into the water. On all fours, he crawled to the side and looked at the ripples where Max had gone under

The shark continued to circle the raft.

Polly and Amanda stood on the sidewalk in front of the store for a moment, while the mother consulted her list of errands. "Ah, vacuum bags," she uttered, and moved down the row of stores to Cheaper Sweepers, Amanda at her side.

"Are we going to Sally's house today?" the doll asked.

"No, the party's not till tomorrow," Polly said before realizing that wasn't her daughter's voice. She glanced down. The baby was half-reclining in Amanda's arms, staring at the mother.

"I don't want to live with Sally," the doll announced. "I want to live with Amanda."

Polly's eyes widened. She covered her mouth with her hand. She stood stock still.

❧

Max didn't surface for what seemed a very long time. He came up sputtering, a tight grip on the fishing net. He swam to the raft and handed the net to his son. "Where's the shark?" he whispered.

"Over there." Jack pointed to his right.

"Move back so I can get onto the raft."

Jack grasped the net and scooted back. He looked from his father to the shark and back again.

Max hoisted himself out of the water and lay on his stomach just long enough to catch his breath before curling his legs and sitting.

Jack threw himself at Max, wrapping his arms around his father's neck. "I thought the shark got you," he cried.

"Not a chance, Buddy." Max peeled his son off him.

"What are you gonna do with the net?"

"Not sure, but I know it will come in handy." Max scanned the debris floating around them, and spotted the rowing oar. It was too far away to get with his hand. But, the fishing net had a telescoping handle. He thought he might be able to guide the oar to the raft with it.

He extended the handle to its full length—about six feet. Hunched on his knees, he inched the net toward the oar, trying to coax it toward them.

It took several tries, but Max was finally successful in capturing the broad end of the paddle inside the net, then slowly, carefully, brought it alongside the raft and plucked it from the water.

He sat back, breathing hard.

"Now what, Dad? How do we get back home?"

"We may have to kill the shark."

"How?"

"I'm not really sure. Let's look at what's floating that might be useful. We don't want to bother with the seaweed, but that piece of driftwood might come in handy. Do you see anything else we could use?"

Jack didn't see how any of the junk floating around them could help. He shrugged his shoulders and said, "I dunno. I never saw a real shark."

"I'm certain you still haven't. Remember, this is a game. But, we have to treat the shark like it is real."

"I saw a guy on the news who got bit by a shark. That shark ate his whole arm. Can't we just row away from it?"

The shark continued to circle the raft, coming closer with each revolution. It was almost close enough for Max to reach out and touch.

"What if we hit it with the oar?" Jack asked.

"Hmm, that's a good idea. I don't know if we can hit it hard enough, but we can try." Max took up the oar, lifted it over his head and waited until the shark came alongside the raft. He brought down the oar on the animal's head as hard as he could.

The shark was stunned and sank.

Max lowered his arms, still holding the oar and watched the ripples. There was no sign of the shark.

"Do you see him?" Jack asked

"No." Max turned around, scanning the ocean. ""And, we're still in the game." He dropped the oar.

⁓

Abruptly, Polly turned and went into Kreate a Koala. Amanda followed at a trot, clutching the doll to her chest.

They went to a bin filled with partially made animals. Polly grasped the baby's body under the arms, took it from her daughter and shoved the doll deep into the pile.

Muffled cries came from the bin. Polly pushed the doll down until she felt the bottom, and heard not a sound.

Silent tears slid down Amanda's cheeks and her nose began to run.

Polly rummaged in her purse, and thrust a tissue at her.

"Why, Mama?" Amanda sobbed. "Why did you do that to the baby?"

Polly knelt in front of the girl. "I don't think she's a very nice baby. "

"Oh, but she is, Mama. I know she is." The girl wiped her eyes and looked pleadingly at her mother. "Please, can't we get her out and take her home?

Polly placed her hands on Amanda's shoulders. "Under no circumstances is that doll coming home with us." She dropped her arms and stood. "Now, what animal do you think Sally would like?"

Max and Jack had been sitting quietly while the raft drifted.

"Dad," Jack said excitedly, lifting himself to his knees. "Dad, look." He pointed toward the horizon. "What's that?"

Max squinted. There was definitely something at the horizon. It was a long way from where they sat, but that black shape could be land.

They would need to propel the raft towards whatever it was. But how? They had only one oar

He looked at the debris floating nearby and espied the driftwood. Once again employing the fishing net, Max guided the narrow plank to the side, and lifted it onto the raft.

"Do you know how to use this?" Max asked, handing the oar to his son

"I think so." Jack took the oar, but kept his gaze on his parent.

"Sit facing that thing out there. When I say 'stroke,' you move it front to back, lift it up and put in back in the water in front of you. I'll do the same with this piece of wood."

"Okay. I guess." There was a note of doubt in Jack's voice.

"We're gonna row to that whatever-it-is," Max announced, taking up his position alongside his son.

"Stroke," Max called out.

The raft moved forward.

"Stroke," he said again.

The rowing was awkward at first, but as they found their rhythm, they found themselves propelling through the water at a fair clip.

The dark mass grew larger. After what seemed hours,

Max and Jack could see it was an island, and rowed with renewed vigor

ॐ

Amanda pondered which animal Sally would like. She already had four bears, a unicorn, and a frog.

The zebra was too stripy. The spider, too leggy. The giraffe's neck was too gangly—at least before it was stuffed.

She picked up a hippopotamus. Its gray plush was soft and silky. Its mouth was open just enough to see a few teeth, and looked for all the world as though it was smiling.

Amanda held it to her chest. It was comforting, even without its insides. "This one," she declared, holding it out for her mother to see.

"Aw," Polly said. "So cute."

They took it to the stuffing machine, where an employee filled the hind-end and middle. Then, she handed a red felt heart to Amanda.

The girl kissed the heart, then placed it inside the hippo.

The animal was returned to the stuffing machine, and filled all the way up to the top of its head and tip of its nose.

Upside down—so as to not lose its insides the hippo was carried to a white-haired woman who had a very grandmotherly air about her.

She placed the animal on its side, took up needle and thread, and sewed the last seam on its tummy. Giving the hippo a squeeze, she held it out for Amanda to take.

"I think it needs a bow," Polly mused. "What color would Sally like?"

"Purple," Amanda replied without any hesitation. "Sally

118

loves purple. Even her bedroom is pained purple."

"Purple it is," the seamstress said, and set the hippo on the table. Se twirled her chair around, took a purple bow from a box hanging on the wall, turned around, and sewed the bow right between the hippo's ears.

❧

"Dad," Jack said. "How come the sun hasn't moved?"

Max hadn't noticed, but realized the boy was correct. The sun hadn't moved at all the entire time they'd been trapped in this game. "I don't know. Must be the people who wrote the game wanted it that way."

The words were no sooner out of his mouth than darkness came, like turning off a lamp. Jack looked up to see twinkling stars and a waning moon. "What just happened?"

"Nighttime. It's a game, remember?" Max reached out and squeezed his son's shoulder. "Put your oar between us, lie down and try to rest. We'll start rowing again when it's light."

❧

The hippo was placed in a box and gift wrapped while Polly paid for it.

Pleased with their purchase, they left the store, Amanda clutching the package.

Polly turned right.

"I thought you wanted to get vacuum bags," Amanda said. "It's the other way."

"We'll get them. I think we deserve a treat. We're going to The Doughnut Hole first."

Daylight came as suddenly as the night. Max sat up and looked around, trying to get his bearings. The raft had drifted closer to the island.

Jack rubbed the sleep from his eyes and squinted into the brightness.

"Grab your oar. We're very near land," Max said.

"I'm hungry," Jack complained.

"I know. So am I. We can forage when we get onto the island."

"Where's the shark?" The boy picked up the oar and plunged it into the water.

"Dunno. Haven't seen him since I bonked him on the head."

The pair rowed in silence as they drew closer to land, and the water shallower. Cautiously, Max reached over the side, his fingertips touched the sandy bottom.

They dropped the oar and driftwood and stepped off the raft. The warm water lapped at their legs as they trudged onto the beach.

As soon as they reached dry land, the strange feeling returned and they found themselves sitting in the chairs in the back room of Chuckie's Toy Store.

Charles Baumgartner stood in the doorway, his hands clasped across his stomach. "Did you enjoy the game?"

Jack stood and handed over the game controller. "No. It wasn't as much fun as I thought it would be."

Charles looked to Max.

"It had an unexpected twist. We'll pass on this game." He left the controller on the chair seat, and gazed at Charles. "I need to rethink this whole video game system thing." Max placed a protective arm around his son. "Let's go down to The Green Burrito. I'm starving."

Polly shuddered as they passed in front of Chuckie's Toy Store on their way to Cheaper Sweepers. She glanced in the window and saw the man who had held the door for them earlier. He and the boy looked shaken and unsteady. She wondered what horror had befallen them. The man and boy were near the door. She looked away, silently vowing never to shop at Chuckie's Toy Store again.

But, of course, she did.

The Phoenix Spoon

By Jacque Summers

The bell over the door marked *The Phoenix Spoon* rang as another customer entered the busy store. The woman at the counter, with her swept back grey hair and round face, paid certain attention to this new entrant. She had ignored the couples milling about the wedding spoons, the teens giggling over the love spoons, and the three women surveying the baby spoons. No, this new entrant was special.

The woman set down her carving knife and spoon blank and watched the woman mill amongst the crowd. The young woman wore a raincoat and carried a heaviness to her stroll. As the shoppers milled about, and, as they are wont to do, leave in a pattern, the store emptied to only two occupants.

The shopkeeper smiled at the woman, urging her to look up. Tears balanced on the woman's eyes. With a strengthening larger smile, the shopkeeper convinced the woman to make her way to the counter.

"Hello," the older woman said, "Can I help you?"

With a trembling smile and a wipe of the tears, the younger woman came right up to the counter and leaned in. With trembling hands, she withdrew a spoon from her purse and carefully set it on the counter. It was a baby spoon, meant to celebrate the birth of a child, meant to make life's journey with the individual. The woman recognized it from a batch she made a few years earlier.

"This was purchased for me here," the woman said, trembling. Then she cleared her throat. "I... I will not be using... I mean, I cannot use..."

"Ah," was all the shopkeeper said, but she said it with a knowing tone.

Still tearful, the young woman said, "I know they spent quite a good deal of money on it-"

"But you just can't bear to look at it?" The old woman finished.

For the first time, the younger woman looked up into the eyes of the shopkeeper. Only her eyes, glazed with age and years of knowing exactly how this young woman felt, could tell the full truth.

The young woman dissolved into another bout of crying. "I'm sorry," she said. "This happens at the most annoying times."

"Don't I know," the older woman said. "Tell you what," she continued, "I have an idea." She reached beneath the counter, as if by memory, and pulled out something brown and shiny onto the counter.

"There is no section for this spoon on the wall," she said, "because there is no word in English for a person who has lost a child."

The young woman sniffed and whined a little, halting her tears.

The old woman smiled again.

"I carved this from ironwood, the hardest wood on the planet. It was hard, and I gave myself a great scar in doing so," they both looked down at the two-inch silvery scar on the woman's left hand, a hand knotted and marbled by heavy use and age.

"But you know what," the shopkeeper continued, "that is the nature of this spoon." She waved the spoon about.

The old woman opened her hand. The intricately grained wood swooped through the pattern. A bird, rising from flames, flew up from the bowl of the spoon. "It is a Phoenix. A mythical creature. But there were also cracks in the wood. These cracks were filled with gold. The gold made an uneven, strangely patterned river flowing through the spoon.

Do you know what a phoenix is?" The old woman asked.

The young woman shrugged, unsure of the answer.

"The phoenix is a bird that, at a certain moment, erupts into flames and is consumed."

The younger woman nodded, absently, her mind in another place.

But that did not stop the shopkeeper from continuing, "Right now, you are being consumed in the fire. But then, when she is ready, the phoenix is reknit from the ashes of the fire. She is rebuilt, and she rises, beautiful and more powerful, from the bowl of ashes, and flies away."

The silence in the room was warm and golden as the rivered thread in the spoon. The young woman had slowed her tears. The old woman reached over the battered glass countertop and grasped the young woman's hand.

"I will exchange this spoon," taking the previously purchased spoon, "but only in exchange for this one," and she put the Phoenix spoon in the woman's empty hand.

The young woman pulled away for a moment, but the old woman held firm.

"It's too much," The young woman said automatically. "That is gold, isn't it?"

"It is. The method is called *kintsugi*. In Japan, a thing, even when broken, still has value. It is repaired with gold and becomes even more valuable."

"That is you, and your experience," the shopkeeper said. "It is a rare thing nowadays but I know how it looks...because, you see," and the woman reached back under the counter and withdrew another item, "it matches my own."

And with that, the shopkeeper withdrew another Phoenix spoon, one obviously worn with years of handling. It fit in the old woman's hand like a dream.

The young woman gasped.

"Let me guess," the shopkeeper said, "you feel alone in your loss. You feel like there is no one else out there who can fully understand what you are hearing in your mind, what you are feeling in your heart. They can't understand how your body hurts."

The young woman's eyes were large and limpid by now.

"I know, now you feel that you would do anything to not remember how you feel right now. But that is a false choice. You cannot become the Phoenix if you don't go through the fire.

The fire will consume you. You will come out of the ashes. You are strong. Sometimes, we need a tool, an item to focus our goals on. Same with our worries."

Whenever you feel that the fire is too strong, take out this spoon, and rub the details. As you rub, the edges will smooth and soften, like the pain. You will remember that there is something out there, something strong that will hold you, until you are strong again. Your worries and pains will seep into the spoon, and someday, you will look at the spoon, hanging on the wall, and feel not pain, but the memory of the journey you overcame."

The younger woman shook her head, as if by denying the spoon she was denying the truth of the journey.

The shopkeeper insisted. "You will never unfeel the pain, but you will value it. And you would be surprised how a little spoon could contain all that loss. But somehow, it does." The woman unconsciously rubbed the handle of her spoon.

In a distant voice, the young woman asked, "Can I feel your scar?"

Surprised, and then surprised by being surprised, the old woman smiled and nodded.

The young woman reached out and felt the silver scar on the surprisingly warm hands. Then the young woman looked around. For the first time, she let her eyes drift to the birthday spoons, the love spoons, the anniversary spoons, and the retirement spoons. Her lip trembled just a second, and then she smiled, a huge smile that showed she had changed her mind, that she could breathe again.

The shopkeeper smiled as she wrapped up the Phoenix spoon, "You will find that you are not the same person who came in here this morning. It was brave for you to come at all, to leave your house at all, to leave your sorrow. Your first steps that led you here are now leading you further on."

The young woman took the small bag with the spoon safely wrapped inside. For the first time in their interaction, for months in fact, the young woman smiled. With a wordless wave, she left the store. The bell rang as she exited. Her shoulders were lighter now, and she looked to the sky to see the rain coming. With a smile, she pulled up her hood and was gone.

Behind, in the store, a sound seemed to fill the air, but the shopkeeper knew what it was. It was her *magic,* her magic cast through her spoons. With a soft chuckle, she picked up her carving knife and went back to work.

RETAIL SPACE

AVAILABLE

North Point Mall
on the northeast corner of
the intersection of
Major and Minor Streets

555.732.2666

for more information

Three Bros Gym
The Gym Next Door

By A. K. Antheson

I walk by the storefronts lining the shorter leg of the ell that forms North Point Mall. "Inside the corner of Major and Minor," people say. Sounds like a joke, but there really was a J. B. Minor in the local history.

I always park on Minor, so I can stroll casually, pretending to window-shop the displays, but in truth I know them by heart. Every crack and crevice in the dusty sidewalk is familiar.

At first, months ago, the shop owners eagerly flocked to the windows, but soon, after many days and many passes, they realized I would always look and never buy.

Nutshell caption of my life: always looking, never buying.

But not today. Today would be different.

I linger by the antiques and pawn shop. Always something fresh there, always some castoff, consignment, or genteel pawning. No one comes to the window. They stay in the shadows, sipping the coffee, tea or bourbon that soothes the boredom of their lives.

The spicy scent of Mexican tempts me on my way. Perhaps I'll take him there? No. Tamales only at Christmas, and the guys always eat there. Somewhere special. Maybe that new French café down on Pine.

I walk on toward my goal just past the elbow of the ell, past the narrow passageway to the back alley, to the vacuum store.

It has changed its name a couple of times since my first furtive survey of the mall: 'Cheaper Sweepers,' then 'Economy Vacuums,' now they cover both with 'Cheaper Sweepers—*Economy Vacuums.*'

I ignore the glares from the salesmen inside, the portly owner, and especially the uptight assistant with his gray suit and yellow bow-tie.

❧

Early on, they were all smiles when I had pretended to admire the vacuum cleaners in the window, but of course I was more interested in the gym next door.

The gym next door, with its fantastic window display. Spotless glass, brightly lit interior, and mirrors all along the far wall reflecting the magic inside.

Guys, all twenty-something with a few nineteeners like me thrown in. A lot of pretty, pretty boys I would love to call my friends. We'd find a courtyard to dance in, and always, always dance to remember.

After many days of cowardly retreats I finally walked inside and breathed deep the intoxicating scent of summer boys and their sweet, sweet summer sweat.

This wonderland overwhelmed me with its kaleidoscope of motion and the rustling, rattling, clanking sounds of men on weight machines, treadmills and bicycles that went nowhere.

A gorgeous guy came up to me. He was stacked and well packed. I fluttered a little.

He stuck out his fist. "Hi. I'm Shon Gill."

I almost jumped back, then remembered I was supposed to tap his hammer hand with my dainty knuckles. "Carl Adrian," I admitted.

"You want to join 'The Three Bros Gym'?"

Maybe I could say, 'Just looking.' Or, 'May I watch from the sidelines?' "Uh, yeah."

The other two bros came up and introduced themselves: Shon's brother Mike and their cousin Jim Lee. Shon was twenty-three, Jim twenty, and Mike was an old man of twenty-five.

Mike looked me up and down. "Don't worry. You're in sorry shape, but we'll get you trim in no time. You can start in your street clothes, but you'll want to get outfits like ours." All three wore azure and navy Spandex uniforms that barely contained them.

So I became a gym-boy, but I was along mainly for the view. I was smitten with Shon. There were a lot of nice guys to watch, and some gals too, but the bros were the stars. Mike was chunky beef, Shon was finely chiseled, and Jim was sleek and slim and natural.

I felt naked in my Lycra. Kinda liked it.

Mike would check on me as I worked out. "You're still sorry, but looking better."

Shon kept after me to do weights free-style.

After watching some of this one day, Jim walked over and whispered, "Shon is old school. Do what you want. We're just here to help." He smiled. He always smiled, a little to the left, like his smile was trying to catch his dimple, which always dodged. His eyebrows arched with the smile like a seabird's span soaring above the dancing ocean of his gray-green eyes.

ॐ

Some days later I was on the treadmill, just ambling, watching Shon. His hair was blond streaked and wavy-curled, casually wind-blown like a land-locked surfer dude.

I wondered how long it took him to get that careless, uncombed look.

I realized I'd been staring at Shon a little overtime, so I shifted my gaze to Jim on the treadmill to my right. His rogue hair tousled more naturally, as if he had raked his fingers through it while running out his front door.

He noticed my field inspection, and pink tinged his dodging dimple. His color changes would do a chameleon proud.

He studied the floor between us. "I lost my comb."

"Every day, or just on Thursdays?"

He smiled at me from beneath his bird-wing brows. "Just today. Most times I forget to bring it." His eyes smiled too, until the pink tinge reached the part-time dimple on the right and he broke gaze.

Mike and one of the regulars strode from the locker room laughing and joking. They were dressed in street clothes, and as they passed by, their fingers touched.

Jim watched wistfully as they left. "They're out for some cheap thrills. Gotta love them cheap thrills."

He caught my shocked expression and frowned, his brow more a line of storm clouds gathering. "They're going dancing. What did you think I meant?"

It was all too obvious what I thought he meant.

He leaped off the treadmill and ran to the back.

Shon was squatting a hundred when Jim ran by him. He slammed the weights down on the mat. "Carl, what did you do?" he roared, and tore off after Jim. The look Shon threw over his shoulder at me would have felled a buffalo in full charge.

I had mortally insulted all three without saying a word.

It was weeks before I dared go back. I marched right up and said, "Mike, I'm uncouth, uncool, uncalled for, as well as gutter-butter. I never heard of cheap thrills before. I took the wrong spin. Sorry."

"About what I told the guys. Said you were jerky too."

"Thanks for that."

"We look out for each other. They might've overdone it a little." He yelled in the general direction of the locker room. "Hey, bros. Carl's back and sorrier than ever."

That was a while ago, and things are better than fine now. I'm even doing a little weightlifting free-style just to please

Shon.

And today, today I've got up the gumption to make my move.

I nod to the vacuums and step into my Paradise, the gym next door.

Mike hops up from the baseball game he was watching. "Hi, Carl. You ready for a real—wait, you didn't bring your gym bag."

"I'm not here for a workout. I—I'm here to see...him." I mumble the last part. "I thought...lunch...get to know... better..."

Mike chuckles. "Am I supposed to be surprised?" He lowers his voice. "Ever since you started coming here, he's worked through his lunch break so he wouldn't miss you. I thought you ought to know."

Flattering, but not quite accurate. Shon wasn't always—

"He's got stars in his eyes for you!" Mike says as he sprints toward the back, leaving me to ponder that flamboyant statement.

Mike closes the door, but I hear the louder half of the conversation from the locker room. Mike's half. "What do you mean, you're not ready? You can't pine over a high school crush forever."

I'll say. Shon's twenty-three.

"Just pull your street pants over. You gotta move on. Carl likes you, he can't keep his eyes off of you, and you know you like the guy."

That seems to end the argument. The door opens and Mike gently pushes him out. Him.

The wrong him. Jim. Or Gem, as the jacket that he pulls

on to go into the outside world proclaims. I almost blurt out that there's been a mistake. Then I see him, really see him.

He comes to me, rushing a little, a bashful half-smile, half-grin on his blushing face. His eyes glisten with a shy pride that I would choose him.

Lordy, Lordy, he does have stars in his eyes.

This is what is, and I have to play it the way I find it. A tremblor of the soul shakes my world and changes it forever. I take my feelings for Shon and press them deep back like the gaudy shirt you know you'll never wear. And I'll never tell Gem, or anybody. No after dinner story of How We Met. Not the real story.

A mistake. Yes. But the right mistake. I can see that in his eyes.

I hold out my hand to the boy I choose to love.

Cheaper Sweepers
An Unpleasant Man

By A. K. Antheson

Almost opening time at Cheaper Sweepers. *Gotta get there before Boss Man Corrigan. Vacuum cleaners don't sell themselves.*

Someone's blocking me. An unpleasant man. Cheap, threadbare suit and dirty face. *Get out of my way, I'll be late.*

Just get by him. "Please, I have to open the store." *I hope he doesn't want money.*

"Don't have time for me, Fancy Pants?" His dirty, sallow face thrust into mine, taunting me.

He's down. I struck him without thinking. Mrs. Bauer is watching, her hand to her mouth in shock. *I'm shocked too.*

"So sorry! I don't know why I did that. Here, let me help you."

Up from the sidewalk, on his feet.

"Wow! That was a really good shot—want to try another?"

Again he thrusts his face into mine, and again I knock

him down.

Mr. Cohen, the jeweler, stops trying to park his car and frowns at me.

Sallow-Face, how did you make me do this, assault a stranger in front of two witnesses?

Get away from him. Run around the corner to the back entrance of the store.

Mr. Corrigan is already here.

"A crazy man is following me." My heart is pounding. "Don't let him in."

"We have to open the store in one minute," Boss Man splutters.

We enter. I shut the door and lock it.

"Just don't let him in." I watch Corrigan from the door of the office as he walks through the showroom to the front entrance.

Sallow Face is waiting. He says something I can't hear. Corrigan lets him in.

Slam the office door, crash the exit bar and run out the back to the gym next door. I beg the guys in the locker room to keep Sallow Face out.

Three burly guys, but he brushes by them and comes in anyway.

Bang shut the locker room door. *Scram.* Through the gym and out the front.

Up the street, stay close to the storefronts. Try to keep out of sight of the gym.

Running by the park. *Innocent families are playing. Can't lead that madman there. I should warn them, but what could I say? An unpleasant man is chasing me? They might think I'm the psycho.*

A police car just up the street.

Two patrolmen. One, the driver, ram-rod straight, the other, pudgy, munching a doughnut.

Pounding on the squad car window. "Help! A crazy man is chasing me."

The chubby one rolls it down. "Hey, lay off the glass! What's wrong?"

"He . . ." *Just what did he do?* "He was rude to me." *Very lame.* "He stuck his face right into mine. I hit him—"

"You hit him?" Doughboy drops his doughnut into the box and starts taking notes. "What else did you do?"

Back off, nice and easy. "Nothing. It was just a misunderstanding. Don't worry about it."

The radio squawks and Ramrod answers the call. Doughboy jams his notebook into his pocket and glares at me. The squad car takes off with lights flashing and siren screaming.

A bus pulls over and stops. *Metro to the rescue.* I'm first in line.

The doors fold open and Sallow Face gets off.

Through the park running hard. *I don't care about anybody else now. He's right behind me.*

Out into the street. Brakes screech. Car hits me. Didn't see it.

Can't move. Broken in the gutter.

People's faces blot out the sky. Sallow Face breaks through and throws himself on my dying body, driving my broken ribs deep into my ruptured lungs.

Is this the last thing I see, your ugly face, your wild eyes staring into mine? Is this the last thing I feel, your hand clutching at me, clawing for my wallet? Your voice, the last thing I hear?

"My brother, my brother, you killed my brother!"

The Green Burrito

By Ronn Couillard

This is a story of the great bungled robbery pulled off by three geniuses, best referred to as the hapless trio.

Located in the far corner of the North Point Mall there is a small Mexican restaurant called The Green Burrito. It is a popular eating establishment and does a reasonably good business.

This is a story about an incident that occurred at The Green Burrito and illustrates an age-old and well-known proverb. In general, that proverb is set forth as: "Don't bite off more than you can chew." While the meaning would seem to relate to the necessary activity of consuming food, it can, and has been, applied to other human endeavors.

Once upon a time three would-be robbers, who could well be described as the hapless trio, decided to commit the perfect crime. The three, known by their nicknames as Shorty, Weezer, and Fats, were not what one would refer to as master criminals. In fact, they were not "master" at anything, but did have delusions of grandeur. These delusions led them to believe that if they committed the perfect robbery, one where they got away with a large amount of money and couldn't be identified, that they would become famous. They not only would have some money to spend, but would also have bragging rights and respect from their other loser buddies.

Shorty, a loquacious simpleton, was the brightest of the three, which isn't saying much. It was he who devised the master plan, and being the silver-tongued dolt that he was, had no trouble selling it to his two buddies. It was decided that they would remove the day's proceeds from Shorty's place of employment. It seems that Shorty had no special allegiance to his employer, even though it was one of his longer jobs—he had been employed there all of three weeks. Tired of having to get out of bed and go to work, he concocted a brilliant scheme wherein he and his two companions would "hit the place" at closing time.

"The place" was The Green Burrito. While working there as a dishwasher, the ever-observant Shorty had noticed that at closing time, which was around 9:00 p.m. on weekdays, the procedure was for the crew to clean the restaurant. While this was being done, the manager would take the day's receipts to the office, count them, and then take them to the bank for night deposit.

Shorty's ingenious plan called for the three of them to drive to The Green Burrito, park in the alley behind the building, and don disguises. Shorty astutely reasoned that he might be recognized, thus the disguises. It was this astuteness that greatly impressed Weezer and Fats.

The plan called for them to enter, with weapons drawn, through the back door of the restaurant which opened onto the alley. Once inside, Weezer and Fats would hold the employees at bay, while Shorty would go to the office and take the proceeds. They would then flee out the back door to their waiting car and make a successful getaway.

On a Thursday night in mid-April they were prepared to put their plan into action. Weezer, the only one of the three who had a car, drove them to the shopping mall. The North Point Mall consists of two single-story buildings in an L-shape. All the shops in the mall face a large parking area. An alley runs behind each of the mall buildings. The Green Burrito is located at the ninety degree angle where the two buildings meet. Following the plan, Weezer parked the car in the alley a few shops down from The Green Burrito.

All three donned their disguises which consisted of Halloween masks and ski caps. This proved to be somewhat ineffective for Weezer. He had done some boxing and had taken so many left hooks to the nose, it had been broken several times. The result was that when he breathed through his nose, either in or out, it created a strange whistle. Thus the name Weezer. Wearing a mask would disguise his face, but would have no effect on his strange whistle.

Stealthily they made their way from the parked car, across the alley to the back door of the restaurant, careful not to be seen. So far, so good. The plan was working.

Upon reaching the back door the first unaccounted for obstacle confronted them—the door was locked. But, not to be deterred, Shorty knocked on the door. Someone from inside asked, "Who is it?"

Shorty answered, "It's me, Shorty." He wasn't what one would refer to as a quick thinker.

The door was opened by one of the employees who knew Shorty and recognized his voice. The three robbers then burst through the open door waving their guns about and shouting, "Everyone get against the wall."

Now, it just so happened that this was a very clean restaurant, and the employees routinely mopped the floors every night at closing time. This mopping was under way in the hallway at the time the bumbling three made their entry. In accordance with the plan, Weezer and Fats held the employees at gunpoint and Shorty began running down the hallway toward the office to get the loot. Never known as a particularly agile individual, he lost his footing on the slippery, wet floor. Both feet went out from under him and he fell smack down onto his wallet. As he hit the floor the gun he held in his hand discharged toward the ceiling. The bullet struck the overhead light fixture, and the hallway became dark. Shorty had shot out the lights.

Undaunted, Shorty scrambled to his feet and raced to the office. He burst through the office door, stuck his gun in the face of the startled manager, and yelled, "Ruben, don't make a false move. Put all the money in a bag and give it to me."

Of course, Ruben was Shorty's boss and knew his voice, which was another little obstacle Shorty had overlooked. Nevertheless, with this clumsy oaf waving a gun around, Ruben's better judgment told him to simply follow directions, and maybe Shorty could get himself and his cohorts out of the restaurant without any more damage being done.

While all of this was going on, Weezer and Fats obtained the key to the back door from one of the employees. Shorty came from the office with the bag of money and the three left out the back door. Fats then used the key to lock the door from the outside as Shorty's plan had called for. These three rocket scientists figured they would lock the employees inside the building while they made their getaway. It never dawned on them that the door *unlocked* from the inside.

Once outside, the three bandits removed their disguises. They placed them into a dumpster that was adjacent to the back door. They then ran across the alley and down to their car.

When they reached the car, yet another problem arose. It seems that in all the haste and excitement, Weezer had locked his keys in the car.

However, even such an unexpected occurrence couldn't deter this master criminal. He swung his fist, which held the gun, at the driver's side window. The gun barrel struck the window, shattering and breaking it. At this same time the gun went off and shot a hole through the windshield. A small area of the driver's side window was broken out and Weezer stuck his hand through this small opening to reach the door lock. He was able to unlock the door, but while doing so cut his forearm to the extent that it bled profusely.

Now it seems that Weezer got squeamish at the sight of blood, especially his own. And wouldn't you know it, Weezer got woozy and passed out right next to the car. There this would-be bandit lay prone on the ground, gun in hand, arm bleeding, eyes closed, and making those strange whistling sounds.

Shorty and Fats picked up Weezer and managed to get him into the back seat of the car. Shorty then drove to his house whereupon he made a startling discovery—they did not have the bag of money with them! In their haste to discard their disguises into the dumpster, Shorty had inadvertently dropped the bag of money in there also.

With the assurance that their brilliant tactic of locking the employees inside the restaurant would give them time to return and retrieve the bag of money, they again piled the now conscious, but still groggy, Weezer into the back seat of the car, and drove to the restaurant. Again they parked in the alley a few shops down from the restaurant, leaving Weezer lying on the back seat. Then Shorty and Fats stealthily made their way across the alley to the dumpster.

With Fats serving as a trusty lookout, Shorty lifted and pushed open, the heavy, metal dumpster lid. He then bent over at the waist into the dumpster to look for the elusive money bag. At this point it needs to be pointed out that, just like his two cohorts, Shorty's nickname fit his physical description. He was a short guy. In fact, he was so short that when he bent over the edge of the dumpster to reach inside, his feet were far off the ground. While leaning in and feeling around with both his hands inside the dumpster, he found the bag and joyfully hollered out, "I found it."

At this time, Fats had his back to the dumpster while watching the alley way for anyone approaching. Upon hearing Shorty say he had found the money bag, Fats, still with his back to the dumpster, reached down and grabbed the lid. He lifted it and slammed it shut.

Unfortunately, when Fats slammed the lid down, Shorty had not yet exited the dumpster. He was still bent at the waist with his feet off the ground, and leaning into the dumpster. When the heavy lid was slammed shut, its weight on Shorty's backside served to trap him in that position. So there he was—bent at the waist, with his feet well off the ground, held in place by the heavy metal lid, and unable to move. Shorty was effectively held prisoner by the dumpster.

Then Fats, who came by his nickname because of his unique physique—he was about five-foot five and weighed a conservative two hundred and sixty pounds, sort of a Mr. Five-by-Five—began running to the car to make his getaway. However, as luck would have it, when he closed the dumpster lid, he had spread his feet wide apart and bent over to reach down and grab the lid. This action put an overwhelming pressure on the top button fastening his pants and caused it to snap off. Because of the missing button there was no support protecting the zipper. The pressure of the huge, bouncing belly and the large thighs moving back and forth as he ran, caused the zipper to completely rip open. This in turn caused the fleeing Fats to lose his britches. They just fell down to his ankles flipping him ass-end over tea kettle.

The restaurant employees heard the commotion and ran to Fats. He was flopping around like a fish out of water, trying to get to his feet, but unable to do so because of being tangled up in his pants. Needless to say, he was a rather easy capture. The police, who had already been called, arrived and took the half-dressed Fats into custody.

The employees pointed out the hapless trio's car to the

police. It was still parked in the alley. Upon searching it, the police found the still woozy Weezer lying on the back seat. The bleeding had stopped, but he was still making those strange whistling sounds. They took him into custody. He also was a rather easy capture.

They then began the search for the "brains" of the outfit, Shorty. About this time a muffled call of "Help" was heard from the area of the dumpster. Sure enough, there was Shorty still bent over into the dumpster. He was securely held in place by the heavy lid and unable to move. When the police finally extracted him, he was still clutching the bag of money that the trio had so ingeniously stolen. Just like his other two bandit-buddies, he was a rather easy capture.

This abortive attempt to commit the perfect robbery is still talked about today by the employees of The Green Burrito. Each time the story is told, it makes abundantly clear that there are some individuals who are just not well suited for a life of crime.

Ruby's Antique-Pawn Shoppe

By Newell G. Bringhurst

How did I ever find myself in this situation, Stanley Ruby lamented to himself as he sat alone behind the counter of his well-stocked Antique-Pawn Shoppe, tucked away at the far end of the North Point Mall. Ruby was irked by the recent opening next door of "Cohen Family Jewelry Store," whose line of merchandise—fine jewelry and name-brand watches—duplicated similar items in his own establishment.

Making matters worse, Stanley had just been confronted by Nathan Cohen, the jewelry store's owner-proprietor. Cohen was enraged over a statue in Ruby's shop window featuring a Nazi Spread Eagle clutching a German Swastika Flag.

"What kind of a Jew are you retailing such obscene garbage?" Cohen bellowed. "Have you forgotten that both our fathers suffered through the horrors of the Holocaust?"

Cohen continued, with increasing anger, "Over the years, I have regretted knowing you, I have questioned your commitment to our Jewish heritage and all that it stands for." Waving his finger in Stan's face, Nathan yelled, "I have often wondered, if you are really Jewish. What kind of a Jewish name is 'Ruby,' anyhow?"

Suddenly, without giving Ruby a chance to reply, Cohen stormed out the shop, slamming the door so hard, that the offending Nazi statue wobbled perilously on its base. Ruby rushed over to prevent the tottering artifact from crashing into pieces onto the floor.

Wow, what would have happened if Cohen, had noticed all of the other World War II Nazi memorabilia that I am offering for sale?

⅋

Stanley Ruby's unsettling confrontation with Nathan Cohen was very much on his mind when later that evening he visited his elderly father, Jacob, a resident of the Four Creeks Assisted Care Center.

Jacob Ruby was the original proprietor of Pawn Shop that his son had taken over following his own retirement some years earlier. Up to that time, father and son, had operated the business jointly, gradually expending beyond the usual pawned items—jewelry, watches, musical instruments, and electronics. Now it included works of art, upscale artifacts and historic memorabilia. Such higher-end merchandise was featured in a special antiques section of the shop.

"Like father, like son," grumbled Jacob, in response to his son's description of the encounter with Nathan Cohen. "I know, all-too-well, his impossible father, whom, unfortunately, I first met back in the 1940s."

The conversation continued as Jacob and Stanley shared a late evening meal in the Four Creeks dining room.

"As German Jews, Abraham and I both miraculously survived the horrors of the Holocaust while confined at Auschwitz. We barely knew each other during that awful period."

Jacob was vague in providing details on how the pair managed to survive their years of extreme deprivation at Auschwitz—the most notorious of all Nazi camps. Auschwitz's major function was destruction of the Jewish race—Adolf Hitler's "Final Solution to the Jewish Problem."

"Abraham and I actually got to know each other in New York City following the end of World War II. At first, we were pretty good friends, given our common heritage and interests," Jacob reminisced, wistfully.

"We formed a partnership opening a pawn shop in Harlem. But our association proved short lived. He behaved like a Shylock—straight out of Shakespeare's 'The Merchant of Venice.'"

"I angrily left New York, hoping never to see Cohen again. But alas, he was destined to pop up again in my life—like a dirty, unwanted shekel."

At that point, Stanley asked, "That was when you moved out to Utah, wasn't it? What compelled you to settle amongst all those Mormons?"

"Well, it is a long story. Immediately after my falling out with Cohen, and being down and out, I was befriended by a pair of young, clean-cut Mormon missionaries. Their ulterior motive was to convert me to their faith. They proclaimed the

Latter-day Saints—as they call themselves—to be the new 'chosen people,' akin to our Jewish ancestors. As God's most favored, they further asserted, Mormonism was destined to save the world from the ravages of the approaching End Times. Although I rejected their efforts at conversion, I was impressed with the missionaries' straight-forward honesty and earnestness combined with the faith's emphasis on the closeness of family and in helping one another in times of need."

"Thus, acting on impulse, I suddenly packed up my belongings and moved to Mormonism's 'Zion in the Mountain West.' I was also drawn by Utah's distinctive geography remarkably like that of our own Israel. Its major fresh water lake, Utah Lake is like the Sea of Galilee, whose outflowing river, called the Jordan, drains north into its own Dead Sea—the Great Salt Lake. I was also aware of Mormonism's record of relative tolerance toward Utah's small, visible Jewish minority.

"But, father," Stanley immediately broke in, "I distinctly recall your telling me of your trials in adjusting to life amongst the extremely clannish Mormons. All of this prompting you to flee, after less than two years."

"Yes, that is true," Jacob replied. "But I am extremely grateful for the experience. I was able to establish my first successful pawn shop in Salt Lake City. More important I met and married my sweetheart, your wonderful mother. Except for that, you would not be here today."

"That's true," Stanley agreed. "You have to admit that it was a very difficult courtship, given that mother grew up in a stalwart Mormon family."

"But as you are well-aware," Jacob quickly replied, "she rejected the tenets of the LDS faith when she came of age, choosing instead to convert to Judaism as our relationship became more serious. That we were married in a Jewish Synagogue rather a Mormon Temple, infuriated both her immediate and extended family. Her parents referred to me as 'the grasping, grubby Jewish Pawnbroker' who stole their daughter."

Stanley then wryly noted, "I have heard it said that the Mormons consider anyone not of their faith a 'Gentile' making Utah the only place on the face of the Earth where a Jew is a 'Gentile'"

"Very true," agreed Jacob, with a slight chuckle. Turning serious, he remarked, "All of that made it impossible for us to remain in Utah, prompting our move here to the Central Valley where you were born and came of age."

"Things turned out quite well. I was able to establish a successful pawn shop, and ultimately able to bring you into the business, which led to its expansion into the Antique-Pawn Shoppe that we have today."

"Although my grief is for your mother, gone so young. Congestive heart failure. She was just forty-nine years old." Jacob shook his head, sadly. "Peace be upon her."

One other negative disrupted Jacob's life. The arrival of his old nemesis, Abraham Cohen, lured to California by his close long-time friend, Murray Rosen who had earlier migrated to the state. Rosen, likewise, was a survivor of the Holocaust.

"Soon, thereafter," Jacob recalled bitterly, "Cohen and Rosen set up a competing pawn shop close to my own—then located downtown on Main Street. They sought to drive me out of business, which obviously failed. This all occurred prior your entering into partnership with me, and our subsequent move to the North Point Mall."

"Now his son, Nathan, is obviously pursuing the same objective in establishing his 'Cohen Family Jewelry Store' next door. Clearly old Abraham, himself, is behind all of this. That one-hundred percent Shmuck just never gives up."

&

At that moment, into the dining room walked Abraham Cohen, also a resident of Four Creeks. Jacob and Stanley hoped that Abraham would not notice them at the far end of the spacious room. But to no avail. Cohen charged toward them, spoiling for a fight.

Approaching Stanley, Cohen thrust his finger into the younger man's chest, hissing, "The fact that you are selling obscene Nazi artifacts in your two-bit establishment angers me. But it doesn't surprise me, given that you are not authentically Jewish. Your late mother was never really Jewish, despite her so-called conversion away from that damnable Mormon religion. At best, you are a 'half-breed Jew.'"

The increasingly agitated Cohen, then turned on Jacob, confronting him face to face: "You are responsible for your half-breed son's lapse from our proud Jewish heritage, given your own behavior in rejecting the most important part of your Jewish heritage—your family surname "Rubenstein" proudly borne by your forebearers. I suspect you chose the name "Ruby" for crass business reasons, reflective of your entry into the pawnbroker business. 'Ruby's Pawn Shoppe'— what a clever play on words."

"Or perhaps" Cohen continued, "in choosing that name, you were enamored with your near-namesake, Jacob "Jack" Ruby —the Dallas mobster, turned strip club owner, who let JFK assassin Lee Harvey Oswald have it in the gut on live television back in '63? You have certainly embraced Jack Ruby's disreputable business practices."

"Stop, Abraham, you are being absolutely absurd. My father, was always completely fair and ethical in his business dealings, unlike yourself."

Abraham shouted at Stanley, "You want to know the truth about your dear father? How he survived the horrors of Auschwitz while one million of his fellow Jews were systematically executed in its gas chambers?"

Immediately, an anguished Jacob, spoke up, begging, "Oh, Abraham, please, let's not go there. Let's not dredge up the horrors we both endured."

Ignoring Jacob's pleas, Abraham continued, "Your so-called 'ethical' father managed to survive Auschwitz because of his damnable conduct as a KAPO guard overseeing a prison work force, known as the Forest Team, responsible for harvesting and gathering wood in the nearby forest needed for cooking and heating the camp."

"Among those prisoners, was Murray Rosen—my good friend, who suffered your father's brutal treatment. Murray vividly recalls how your father carried a whip and club which he used to beat those unfortunate workers who failed to meet their prescribed quotas. In return your dear father was given special treatment and allowed privileges denied his fellow prisoners."

"No, that is absolutely false," Jacob quickly spoke up. "Murray was not even a part of the work detail I supervised. He was actually a KAPO guard, himself, overseeing his own labor force, known as the *Sonderkommandos* or Special Forces. Their duty was to actively assist the SS in the execution of prisoners in the gas chambers, and subsequent cremation of their remains. It was Murray who carried a whip and club to make sure those under him carried out this gruesome task.

"As for yourself, Abraham" Jacob further added, "I am quite aware of your role as a KAPO guard, supervising your own detail, the *Goldjuden* or Gold Jews—most of whom like yourself were one-time jewelers. You were all responsible for receiving and sorting the money, gold, and other valuables taken from the arriving prisoners. All of you were the envy of the entire camp, in that it was known that you were siphoning off money and valuables for yourselves, in cahoots with the SS personnel in charge. Thus, you not only survived, but flourished within the confines of your restricted environment. It was there that you perfected the less-than-honest tactics later employed in your jeweler-pawnbroker businesses."

In the midst of this heated exchange, Cohen's son, Nathan entered the room. He had overheard the latter part of conversation, detailing his father's activities during the Holocaust.

The younger Cohen inquired in a shocked voice, "Is that

true father? Or is it another lie concocted by the pseudo-Jewish Ruby clan?"

The elder Cohen, now ashen-faced, broke down sobbing, "Yes, I did unspeakable things I am ashamed of, and deeply regret." He began to beat his fist on his chest in utter sorrow. "It all came down to a matter of survival for those of us who cooperated with the SS in charge at Auschwitz. Alas, the labor provided by the hundreds of KAPO supervised Jewish workers, proved absolutely necessary to the camp's continuing operation.

"Abraham is absolutely correct," Jacob, painfully admitted, fighting back tears of his own. "We actively facilitated the gruesome process of sending thousands of our Jewish brethren and sisters to their deaths."

All four men were now silent, fathers and sons, processing memories and imaginings of unspeakable pain.

Finally, the younger Ruby anxiously asked, "Knowing the ultimate fate of your fellow Jews, what prevented you along with other KAPO leaders from organizing a mass revolt, within the camp? With the knowledge and organizational skills your group possessed, it would seem that such an uprising might have succeeded? At the very least, you could have given your SS overseers a good fight?"

Jacob quickly responded, "Unfortunately, there was no way of organizing the mass of prisoners, given their diverse nationalities. Although 90 percent of the inmates were fellow Jews, they were transported to Auschwitz from not just Germany but from throughout Nazi-occupied Europe—Poland, Hungary, Russia, Italy, France, and the Netherlands. Also imprisoned at the camp were Soviet POW soldiers, non-

Jewish Poles, Roma Gypsies, Jehovah Witnesses, and homosexual males."

Finishing the story, Abraham quickly added, "Thus, Jacob and I focused on just surviving, albeit by any and all means possible. The situation in the camp deteriorated into 'the survival of the fittest' by the time Auschwitz was finally liberated and we were set free."

Ș

The stark disclosure of the details of their imprisonment at Auschwitz proved cathartic for Jacob and Abraham as well as their sons. As a result, the two elderly Holocaust survivors emerged more empathetic and understanding of each another.

Murray Rosen, however, met a different fate, as the specifics of his activities at Auschwitz became known. Shortly, thereafter, he was found dead in his small, squalid downtown apartment—the result of a self-inflicted gunshot wound.

Meanwhile, Stanley Ruby and Nathan Cohen became more tolerant of one another. Both became increasing active in the community's small, but visible Jewish Congregation. Together they sought to inform younger, non-Jewish local citizens of the grim realities of the Holocaust while preaching a message of greater tolerance for not just Jews, but for all individuals regardless of race, religion, and/or sexual orientation.

Stanley Ruby subsequently removed the offending Nazi statue from his shop window, relegating the repulsive artifact to an obscure corner in the antique section.

All such developments, notwithstanding, "Ruby's Antique-Pawn Shoppe" and "Cohen Family Jewelry Store" continued to vigorously compete for the clientele visiting the ever-busy North Point Mall.

Cohen Family Jewelry Store
Storm Past

By Lois Innis

Mr. Cohen distractedly parks in front of his store. He is deep in thoughts that make him frown. On the sidewalk in front of him, a young man who works at Cheaper Sweepers, the economy vacuum store in the mall, strikes and fells an unpleasant looking man.

Seeing violence raises Mr. Cohen's blood pressure. He tells himself, "The nice-looking young man who works here must have had a reason to hit that filthy, sallow-faced fellow. It's not my affair. I have enough problems of my own."

Mr. Cohen is very angry, because, yesterday, when he dropped by the Antique/Pawn Shop next door, he saw a sculpture that included a German swastika flag. He hates that flag! Since he saw it yesterday, family history that his parents told and retold keeps racing through his head.

"Your grandfather was the most prosperous jeweler in Berlin when Hitler took over. The Nazi Storm Troopers confiscated your grandparents' home and their store. They took all of the Cohen art collection, including two beautiful, new paintings by the most famous Jewish artist."

Mr. Cohen remembers hearing, "Marc Chagall was born Moisha Segal in 1887. When he left Ukraine and moved to Paris, he changed his Jewish name to make it sound more French. He was very smart. He sold more paintings that way. Your grandparents bought his colorful work when they were in Paris on vacation." Mr. Cohen's dad had continued. "The art collections that Hitler stole were destined for 'The world's most impressive art museum' that Hitler planned to build. An architect had been commissioned and begun plans for it."

Not only the Cohen art collection disappeared. Mr. Cohen's parents were his only relatives who survived the Nazi era. He wishes that every reminder of Hitler could be obliterated. Ever since he saw the swastika yesterday, he's been storming—gloomy faced and thundering at his family!

Mr. Cohen punches in the store security code on his phone. Inside, he stashes the purse that he carries—inspired by leather purses carried by sturdy Swedish men he met when he was very young. They took diamond training classes in Amsterdam together. Aspiring jewelers spent hours with professional diamond graders, cutters, polishers and setters—learning the four C's: CARAT, COLOUR, CLARITY and CUT. They handled rough and polished diamonds. They learned how to distinguish synthetic from true diamonds and gems. Gemologists drilled them on recognizing quality and advised on selecting the most complementary setting for each colored stone. What a wonderful two weeks! So long ago.

Mr. Cohen extracts costly displays from the large safe. Each day, much must be rearranged. In the window he places birthstone rings—large ones for men, smaller designs for women. When the afternoon sun hits them, they will sparkle. They might catch the eye of casual strollers who could lay-away the perfect ring as a gift for a future birthday or graduation.

One colorful display is Navajo, Hopi and Zuni bracelets and earrings. Their turquoise comes from Arizona mines. When Mr. Cohen makes buying trips to the US Southwest, he often chooses small hand painted bowls created by Indian potters. World visitors, in town to visit giant sequoia trees in the nearby Sierra Nevada Mountains, buy Indian crafts.

Mr. Cohen's anger begins to erode as he goes about his work. He thinks about his life and his wife. At busy times Mrs. Cohen comes to help. She smilingly waits on customers. She tells a client which opals come from Australia or Sri Lanka. She shows lapis rings and earrings from the Andes in Peru and talks about diamond mining differences in Africa and other parts of the world. She shows a golden ankh from Egypt. She knows that many customers backpacked in these countries when they were young. They couldn't afford real jewelry then. Now they can buy a reminder of the fascinating trip taken many years ago.

Mrs. Cohen likes to decorate the store for each season. Inexpensive jewelry can be left in view twenty-four-seven, along with brilliant red valentines, or Easter bunnies or Santas to make viewers smile. People of all incomes wander by the windows and wish a bit.

As the day goes by, Mr. Cohen looks thoughtfully at the displays that surround him. He is proud of their store.

Watches are big sellers now. Citizen brand, created in Japan, is very reliable. The sun, or even electric light, keeps it going—no need to buy batteries all the time. A used Rolex costs thousands of dollars—a new one, more thousands. Mr. Cohen thinks, "Women are buying bigger watches now, and men buy smaller ones. Is evolution making them more alike?"

In the case is a range of beautiful pearls. Fifty dollar synthetic ones feel smooth if you put them in your mouth. A string of thousand dollar matched pearls feels rough. Grains of sand that infiltrated the oyster where each pearl was formed became part of the jewel. The finest strings of pearls have a pinkish tint and sell for two thousand dollars.

Now relaxed, Mr. Cohen thinks, "It's a pleasure to earn a good living handling beautiful things.

Enough of anger about the past. NOW and the FUTURE are what COUNT!"

"It's time for me to smile again. I love being a jeweler. In every past generation of Cohens there were jewelers. Our son wants to come into the business when he finishes college. Now, Antwerp in Belgium has taken over from Amsterdam as the diamond capital of the world. We'll send him there to study—then to Paris for fun."

When Mrs. Cohen comes in the door, he greets her with a smile and a lingering hug. In a few years, the two of them might go to Paris for fun—and perhaps, unknowingly, enjoy some of the art once owned by the Cohen family of Berlin.

Great Gifts Shoppe

By Julie Appelbaum

I fear that sitting here, in George's Great Gifts,
no one will notice me For I am little and set aside;
my rivals almost overwhelm.
"Look at me" silently I plead, but still few come by,
and when they do They go for the usual fare
like tiny ballerinas in Stiff folded tole, who perch atop a toe,
the other leg far outstretched, dressed all in pink
for all the little girls on their special birthdays.

Nothing's ever bought for little boys or for men
in a gift shop it seems: they have to have the shiniest
plastic electronic zapping things, probably from a sports
     shop.
But here we are, the two of us bikers on our bikes;
my bud has a girl on the back, and our detail is perfection,
from the colors of our boots and helmets and jeans,

to the tires and steering wheels and goggles, with
a statement on a plain straight piece on the back that reads,
"The age old urge to run away". Who can resist that?
What guy cannot identify? We all got to break away
    sometime,
Grab some sandwiches and a 6-pack and ride out on the
    open road
So sweet and wide, listening to our tunes, kicking back.

∾

Wait! Someone's picked me up, a woman probably buying
    for her son,
and she's turning me over to read the price tag.
I can almost hear her thinking, "It's nice, but would he like
    it?
It doesn't do anything. Maybe I'll just try the sports
    memorabilia store
A few doors over. Maybe a 49'ers mug instead?" she shrugs
    and moves on by.

∾

It's past time for me to find a place, permanently on a shelf
    somewhere
maybe right over the computer where you could see me any
    time you log in.
Ballerina! What are you thinking? Oh, lady, please come
    back; this waiting
is mortifying, and I crave a dose of daily admiration from a
    permanent owner.

∾

Listen, nothing like the open country backwoods road
 leading nowhere or everywhere,
wherever you choose to go. When the sky is clear and
 wildflowers grow
and levies are full and the sun never stops shining, that's the
 best.
Every motorist in a car that passes by, especially the women
 and the kids
in the back, long to be on my bike, free, hanging on for dear
 life
around the mountain curves; the dad'd be sick with envy,
 too, I know because
all guys want basically the same things: a girl, a beer, and
 power in their legs.

ʤ

Wait! Here she is, back again, and coming straight towards
 me. What do you think?
Will my imprisonment in this dump finally end? I need a
 self-respecting place to be!
Am I to be free at last?
She's checking in her wallet, "Oh, good, I have enough cash
 to buy it outright,
and he'd never know the price. Perfect: I'll buy it!"

ʤ

The salesclerk rings me up asking if she'd like a bag. She
 leaves.
The biggest hurdle's over, now I'm in the car, and she's put
 me on the kitchen
table with a birthday card and here he comes!

Oh, Lord above, will he like me? Help!

"I love it", he says. "I'll put it right on the shelf over the computer.

Thanks, sweetie." He seals his approval of the gift with a kiss. At last.

"Adios, amigos!" yell I, "Adios, and goodbye. So long suckers, all you tiny ballerinas".

The Fix-it Shop
Keeping an Eye on Waldo the Great

By Steve Pastis

Tripping happily along the hot sidewalk was Mr. Bannister, the last in a long line of happy-go-lucky sidewalk trippers dating back to the first sidewalks in Duluth. The current Mr. Bannister carried all of the Bannister traits. He was tall, blond, and used a very silly expression to convey his nonchalance.

Waldo the Great owned a small fix-it shop on the boulevard where Mr. Bannister was continuing family tradition. While Waldo the Great tended to enjoy the sounds of people walking back and forth along the pavement, there was something in the quirky rhythm of Mr. Bannister's footsteps that caused him to walk out of his shop and offer a few loud words.

"Where did you learn to walk?" was the first group of Waldo the Great's loud words.

I didn't have to learn to walk," Mr. Bannister calmly responded. "Walking is in my genes."

"But you're wearing cords," said Waldo the Great.

"Not my pants type of jeans, my heredity type of genes," clarified Mr. Bannister. "Through family traits that have been passed down from generation to generation, I walk the way I walk."

Waldo the Great went back into his shop to find a small appliance to hurl in the general direction of Mr. Bannister. Upon locating a thirty-year-old toaster, he grabbed it only to find that Mr. Bannister was now inside his shop standing very close to the large front window.

"Would you mind moving out to the sidewalk?" asked Waldo the Great politely. "I would like to hurl this toaster at you and I would hate to break my front window."

Responding to the politeness of the request, Mr. Bannister walked out to the sidewalk to have the toaster thrown at him. Not being a fool, Mr. Bannister walked backwards out of the shop to keep an eye on Waldo the Great.

Waldo the Great put the toaster down on a blue wooden rocking chair and shook his head. "That was beautiful," he thought and he asked Mr. Bannister to come back into the shop.

Mr. Bannister walked back into the shop, confused about why the toaster was now on a chair. Waldo the Great screamed and pounded his fist on the counter.

"No, you idiot, not like that!" shouted Waldo the Great. "Walk backwards again."

Mr. Bannister offered no complaints about the request. He was more than willing to walk backwards to once again keep an eye on the cranky repairman.

"That's it!" shouted Waldo the Great. "That's beautiful. Your steps are so melodic when you walk backwards. It's as if all the melody inside you paces your steps when you go backwards. Please do it again."

Mr. Bannister turned to face the door of the shop and walked backwards toward the counter. Upon hearing applause from Waldo the Great, he turned and walked backwards to the door. He repeated the process again and again.

After about half an hour of this, as Mr. Bannister walked backwards to the counter again, Waldo the Great hit him over the head with the toaster, killing him. After dragging his body behind the counter, Waldo the Great found Mr. Bannister's wallet and helped himself to a healthy amount of cash.

Waldo the Great dragged Mr. Bannister's body to a back room where it was placed on top of other bodies. Waldo the Great then walked to his front window to find his next customer.

Beauty Accentuated
A Woman's Salon

By Sylvia Ross

When she stepped down from the bus at North Point Mall, Beth stepped into a small, grassy, rectangular park just at the edge of the sidewalk where two streets came together. The tiny park had a bench with a back to it, and two small trees. There was a trash bin with shiny blue paint, and no trash was on the ground, not even a gum wrapper, or crumpled potato chip bag or a cigarette butt. Two old white guys were setting up a chessboard on the bench. She'd never actually watched anyone play chess, but she recognized the pieces from TV. There was a thermos sticking out of the pack on the ground beside them. Neither of the men had looked up when the bus stopped. She was glad not to be noticed. The little park was cut from the mall's big parking lot. North Point wasn't a huge mall, or new, but its buildings were freshly painted. There was no spray paint or scuffs along the walls. North Point Mall looked clean and safe.

Before Beth crossed the parking lot, she began to scan

the signs above the shops from left to right. Her eyes paused slightly at each of the marquees above the storefronts until they passed the "L" turn where the mall stopped going south and began going west. It boxed the parking lot in on two sides. She kept scanning, and finally found what she was looking for.

The words, *Beauty Accentuated*, were spelled out in vivid coral. Beneath that was a turquoise design, then smaller coral words. She squinted and could read them: *a woman's salon*. It was between a repairman's business and a place that sold potted plants. She took a deep breath.

None of the cars in the parking lot seemed to be over fifteen years old except for a couple of well-maintained classics, an old 1950s Chevy with new shimmering purple paint and fancy hubcaps and an old, vintage VW, also with new paint. She stopped for a moment to admire the VW, then patted the envelope tucked in her shoulder bag, took a deep breath, held it in, then let it out very, very slowly. She'd learned that trick from a nurse in the hospital when she was in labor with Joshua. She felt calmness come over her as the air left her lungs, just as it had a year ago. Joshua came out okay. On this day, she told herself, she would come out okay. She stepped off the grass and onto the asphalt to cross the lines of cars and began walking toward *Beauty Accentuated*.

Most of the vehicles she passed were SUVs. Someday, she would have a car. Not like the Lexus that just stopped to let her cross one of the parking lot's roadways. She wouldn't have to ride a bus anymore. Most of the cars were white. When she was a little girl, cars were more colorful, but since she got into her teens, white had become the most popular color. Here, where there were so many new ones, they almost all seemed to be white.

Her mom believed in signs. Maybe the number of white cars was a bad sign. Maybe it was telling her that she didn't belong here at North Point Mall. Except for two laughing Mexican women getting into one of the white SUVs, the people walking to and from their cars all had skin that ranged from pink to beige. But she had the envelope. Tessa would be embarrassed if she turned around and went home. She would never embarrass Tessa.

An old woman, wearing good clothes, but not new—a jacket when it wasn't cold—was coming toward her holding two big shopping bags. The woman stumbled where the asphalt buckled a little. She didn't fall, but the bag in the woman's left hand dropped to the asphalt. Beth ran forward, bent to pick it up. "Here you go, Ma'am. It's okay. I think nothing got broke."

The old woman had sky-blue eyes in a wrinkly face. She steadied herself and clutching the bag that hadn't fallen, she reached for the bag Beth held. Beth recognized Fabulous Frivolous, a soft dye that lots of the old women who came into Apex chose. "Oh, my dear," the old woman said. "Thank you so much. It gives me much pleasure now-days when young people will go out of their way to be kind."

Beth smiled back, and said, "Take care now. Would you like me to walk with you to your car?"

"No, sweet child. It's right here." She pointed at a white Honda Accord, not the newest on the lot, but not old either. She gave Beth another wide smile and said, "You take care too, dear girl."

As the woman turned to unlock the trunk of her Honda, Beth put her shoulders back and walked on. Maybe she didn't need to be so scared. Maybe this old woman was a good sign. She reached into the shoulder bag and touched the envelope

KayTee Baker was behind her shop's cash register. She was having a bad morning. Six cases of Redken and four of Paul Mitchell product had been delivered already, although it wasn't yet 9:30. She needed to get the boxes opened and product on the shelves, but there had been five phone calls from clients she didn't know who had urgent needs for appointments. One client, Margo Bachelor, had been rudely demanding. Three of the five wanted to come in today, a day she was booked solid. One of her Thursday morning regulars, Sarah, was in the chair, waiting for KayTee to begin her shampoo. Crabby ol' Mrs. Roberts was already here sitting up front, looking at magazines, waiting, a half hour too early. And by 10:30 the next appointment would be in. They'd be overlapping every 45 minutes until 5:30. It was excellent that business was so good, but sometimes she dreamed of selling the shop and taking off to Cabo San Lucas. She'd be happier working as a bartender for minimum wage. She liked Mexican music.

Sandy and Jill, her independent chair renters, booked their own appointments. Jill wasn't in yet and Sandy was as busy as KayTee. Until a few months ago, she'd had two employees in addition to the two renters. But Marge, who'd been with her from her first shop on Washington Road, retired with her husband to the coast last year. KayTee still managed a big clientele with just Patty on half time, until

Patty got a job as a teacher's-aide at her kids' school. KayTee's life had become an exhausting sort of Dante's Hell where she went from sink to dryer to sink to counter to the stink of color dyes from sink to being sad and twice divorced and tired. She could pay her mortgage, shop lease, and do okay. But, she missed the income from those empty chairs that Patty and Marge had filled.

She called one of the women on the scratch pad back. Not Margo *Bitch*elor. She picked a woman who had sounded young and polite, and offered her a 6:45 appointment that evening. Amy Barcellos' was happy to get it, and her name went into the appointment book.

It meant no lunch, and no supper until late. It was a good thing she'd hadn't skipped breakfast. On the scratch pad, there was another woman's name. Her voice had been pleasant and her name seemed familiar. Maybe, she thought, and the thought converted to question. "Sandy, could you squeeze a client in this afternoon?

"Ya. I can. I've had a cancellation. You know Debbie, that long-haired girl who comes in every couple of weeks? She finally went into labor. Her baby is three weeks late. I knew they should have induced..."

"I don't have time for talk," KayTee called sharply from the counter. She grimaced. She'd like her chair renters better if they weren't so chatty. "Yes or no? Her name is Walker and she needs color. Can you fit her in?"

Sandy didn't seem to notice that KayTee was abrupt with her. "Ya. At 2:30, but no later. I have two clients coming after 3."

The salon owner relaxed. Stephanie Walker's name went

into the appointment book for 2:30. KayTee picked up the phone to called her to tell her Sandy would be her beautician when she arrived.

Both of her tenants were good beauticians. They were honest, tidy, cleaned their spots well before they left, took a place at the cash register when customers came in—when she was at a place with a client where she couldn't stop—or had to run an errand. They knew how to push product for the shop's benefit even if it didn't go into their pockets.

Just as she left the counter and went back to finish old Sarah Cox's shampoo and cut, the bell rang over the door. She looked up to find that the silly, annoying young man from the gym. He just didn't get it. He was not welcome in her salon.

"Hi, Miz Baker. Changed your mind 'bout doing my hair?"

The kid wasn't joking. He'd cornered her out in the alley once, making her crazy by asking if she'd take him as a client. There was no way a man was going to ruin the tranquility of her salon. She didn't want to see him here at the counter. "Go away, Shon. Read the sign. *Beauty Accentuated, A Woman's Salon.* Go find yourself a barber."

"But, Miz Baker. You can do exactly what I want. You're right here. I'm not askin' for a discount. I just know you can do exactly what I want. Angela who works at The Doughnut Hole says you did her hair. It's amazing!"

"Out of here. Git."

"C'mon, Miz Baker." He pushed his face forward, and gave her a big-eyed, begging little boy smile. "Please. Angie told me you were about the best in the f-ing city for foil weaves. That's all I want." He hunched up his shoulders half-hanging over the counter. "Please," he begged. I want little golden spikes just like Angie's."

"Out!"

"Please, Miz Baker!"

KayTee's waiting client was taking this all in. That was too much. "Out of here," she repeated.

KayTee lowered her voice. "I don't want to have to have a talk with your aunt, Shon." She felt smug as she watched him leave. He knew she would talk to his aunt. Clara Bauer owned the gym, not her nephews. KayTee didn't like turning down women who could be new clients this morning. But she didn't mind in the least turning down a pushy, muscle-bound hot shot of a young man.

❧

KayTee tipped Sarah's head under the spray. Tessa better be sending me someone dependable and compliant, she thought. She'd hardly begun squirting the shampoo, when the bell on the door tinkled.

She looked toward the front of the salon to see who had come in. It was a tall, black girl with a shoulder pack. This was a surprise customer. *Beauty Accentuated* didn't even stock the kind of product a black girl's hair would need. The girl glanced over the shop quickly, and then sat down on one of the chairs near the front counter, not far from where Mrs. Roberts sat. The girl looked around again, slowly. Her eyes stopped on Sandy, then came to KayTee. The tall girl smiled slightly. OMG, KayTee thought. This must be the girl Tessa promised would come today interviewing for a job.

Sandy, two sinks down, noticed the girl too. She twisted around so that the black girl up in front wouldn't see her face, and she shook her head, 'No." at KayTee. Sandy's pencil-sculptured eyebrows were pinched together as tightly as possible, and she was pursing her lips in a theatrical annoyance. KayTee scowled back at Sandy. It was her shop, not Sandy's. KayTee, as the salon's owner, didn't miss much. She had picked up on the fact that the client in Sandy's chair raised her eyes from the glossy copy of Southern Living when the girl came in. The client, too, had appraised the new girl. But Sandy's client wasn't a dang racist like Sandy. She just went back to looking at the magazine.

KayTee blasted Sandy another look to remind her that she, KayTee Baker, Kathryn Theresa Baker, was the boss, and Sandy was just a tenant lucky enough to even rent a chair at the North Point salon. Then, KayTee gave a gentle pat to Sarah's springy, now foamy, gray-haired head. "Give me a minute or two," KayTee said to her client. She slipped off the latex gloves and went to the front of the salon, hoping that the girl would agree with $15.00 an hour, and a 60-40 split on clients served. As KayTee went forward, she said a prayer that Tessa had come through for her. She'd have some help.

The girl stood up as KayTee approached the front of the salon. KayTee reached out to take her hand, saying, "Hello, I'm KayTee Baker. Are you from the Apex School of Beauty downtown?"

❧

"Yes, Ma'am," Beth said, reaching into her bag for the

envelope. "I am. I'm Beth Jackson. Tessa, oh, I mean Ms. Asadurian, gave me this letter for you."

"We called her Tessa when I was in beauty school too. Beth, I have to get back to my client, but look around, see how we are set up. The bathroom is the door on the right in back. We keep our lockers and supplies through the door to the left. I'll have more time to talk to you in about twenty minutes. If you want to go out and walk around the mall, get something to eat, go ahead, just be back in twenty."

"I'd rather wait here. Is there something I could be doing here while I wait?"

Ah, precious relief, KayTee thought. Lord, you came through for me, but what she said was, "Go to it. There is a cardboard cutter and two tall stacks of boxes back in the supply room. Open the boxes, and you can set up the bottles of product on the shelves behind the counter and over in the corner. The labels will clue you to where the product should go. New product to the back of the shelf, older ones up front. You'll figure it out." KayTee paused, nodded her head toward the supply room. "The locker closest to the window is empty. You can use it for your things. There is a stack of smocks like the one I'm wearing. Don't want you to ruin your clothes, Beth Jackson."

KayTee feeling more optimistic than she had in over a year, grinned. "Beth, huh. Short for Elizabeth?"

"No, Ma'am. Short for Bethlehem."

"Born on Christmas?"

"Two days before, Ma'am. Mary and Joseph hadn't gotten to Bethlehem yet. But it was near enough, so my Mother gave me that name."

"A good name. Oh, you don't need to call me Ma'am. Everyone calls me KayTee. Okay, now, have fun with the boxes. I'll get back to my client. See you in twenty."

The owner of *Beauty Accentuated* watched the tall girl clip the length of the shop and disappear into the supply room. Bethlehem, she thought. She knew there was something good about this girl. KayTee walked back to the sink where Sarah waited for her. Sandy was still glowering, but KayTee knew she'd calm down. Jill, who'd be in at noon, wouldn't even notice the new girl's skin color. She wasn't like Sandy.

Twenty minutes later, Beth — wearing a smock identical to the ones worn by KayTee and Sandy — had opened the boxes, re-stocked the shelves, and was dusting the window sill. KayTee's second client was under an old fixed dryer, so she was free to talk to Beth Jackson. KayTee nodded to Sandy, "Watch the counter. Okay?" then she led Beth out into the back alley. The alley air was tainted by the cars and the trash bins parked along the walls that separated North Point from the subdivisions around it. Still, the trees in backyards gave out oxygen. KayTee took a deep breath, and cleared the salon's chemical smells from her nose and lungs.

"The blue bin is ours, Beth. We never put our waste in any of the others or we have to pay a fine. I'm glad you broke down the cardboard boxes. They take up so much space." KayTee paused to look at the girl as she changed the subject a little. "Do you think you might like working here?"

"Yes, Ma'ma. I do. And, Tessa wouldn't have sent me here if she didn't think it a good place for me."

"Well, I'm a strict boss. I'll expect work for your pay. A

lot of this job is janitorial. You won't just be shampooing, styling, and doing color all day. You'll have to clean the salon, supply room and bathroom, sometimes the alley. I need to know you are competent with those other duties before you'll start working on clients. Then I'll start you out on our older, regulars. If you don't mind." KayTee looked at Beth to make sure that this was acceptable. KayTee herself didn't like working on old women. Beth was nodding her willingness. So KayTee continued. "You'll work the counter too. Working the counter means you sell the product on the shelves, as well as dealing with the cash, checks, and credit card payments. Product is important. It brings in as much money as clients do."

"Really?"

"Yes, we sell the quality lines drug stores don't. Women drive here from all over the city to buy what we stock." KayTee kept talking. "I think you'll be happy enough with the pay. I'd give you a base pay of $15.00 an hour, that's a 9 AM until 5:30 day, with short breaks when you need them, and a half-hour for lunch. On top of the $15 an hour, you'll get a 60/40 split on client money, but you can only keep cash tips." She looked at Beth to make sure the girl was paying attention. "It is just too hard for me to manage the check and credit card tipping.

"60/40 is the standard, and it means you'll have to keep a business log of any client you serve. I'll ask for your log every Thursday evening, so I can have your check made out and ready by Friday morning when you get to work. Does that sound okay?"

"Yes, Ms. Baker. KayTee. It means I'll be getting $120 a

week, minus deductions, plus 40% of client fees and any cash tips." Beth cocked her head and grinned down at her new boss. "Okay."

"You can take your lunch break early on Fridays if you want to get to the bank." KayTee felt relieved Beth was interested in the job. There was more to work out though. "I have some things of my own that I'll expect from you. First, breaks are flexible, but I don't want you to take advantage of that. Also, I don't want you smoking anything in my shop or near it. There is a little park..."

Proudly interrupting, Beth cut in with, "I don't smoke anything, Ma'am."

KayTee was relieved and pleased. "Good," she said. But quickly her face tightened. "Another thing," she said and her voice became brittle. "I don't like men in my place. This is a woman's salon, no men allowed. I don't want any boyfriend or husband or any guy showing up in it, or hanging around in front of it, or waiting for you here in the alley. If some man wants to meet you for lunch or after work, use your phone and arrange where you'll meet. I don't want it to be here."

"KayTee, I'm not married, and the only boyfriend I have or want is my baby boy. He won't be coming to work with me."

"You have a baby?" KayTee hadn't expected that from this young girl. She frowned.

"Yes, Ma'am, I do. He's almost a year old."

KayTee's brows came together. "Well, Beth, I don't want to hire someone who is going to be missing work all the time. Kids get sick."

"Joshua is very healthy, Ma'am. We live with my mom.

She'll take care of him when I'm at work. I promise I'll won't be missing any days."

KayTee glanced at the cars in the alley. "You can't park back here. Sandy and I fill the two slots we're given. The others belong to other shops.

"It's not a problem. I'll be coming by bus."

KayTee was surprised. "Bus?"

"Yes, Ma'am. I don't have a car."

The owner of *Beauty Accentuated* nodded. KayTee couldn't remember talking to anyone who'd ridden a city bus in thirty years. "Oh, one other thing," she said, as she remembered something else that was important. "I've seen too many shops where the beauticians looked like they'd just come off a three-day drunk. I want you to look as well-groomed as you do today always. No tats, and no rings anywhere but your fingers. If you have tats, cover them up. This might not seem fair, Beth, but those are my terms. If you agree, and want the job, you can have it."

KayTee relaxed, stretched, then added, "Oh, I forgot. You'll need to get along with Sandy and Jill, but understand you don't work for them, you only work for me. They are independent space renters. They bring their own supplies and have their own clients, clean up after themselves. They make their own appointments. But we share sinks and dryers. That takes a bit of cooperation on busy days. If this suits you, you are on payroll as of this morning."

"It does suit me, and I promise I'll work hard."

"Sandy takes a bit of getting used to, but she is a good person at heart. She's worked here for eight years. You just have to be a little tolerant. You'll like Jill. She'll be in at noon."

Beth looked quite satisfied with the terms, and KayTee didn't have to fear the prospect of tending bar in Cabo. This girl was tall, slim and classic looking, which would be good for business. And she had a willingness to work hard.

When the two of them went back inside the salon, KayTee Baker beckoned her next client to her chair. Sandy moved away from the counter to prepare for her next client. Beth Jackson looked around. She noticed that a couple of the mirrors had splatter spots, and went to find a bottle of Windex in the supply room. Beth learned how to work the counter that afternoon. Sandy was nicer than KayTee implied, and Jill had greeted Beth with a giggly, huggy welcome. She had gone to Proteus for job help. Its counselors tested her aptitudes and enrolled her at Apex Beauty School. And now she had a real, full-time job. The day had been a marvelous success.

At the end of that day, Sandy was slow to leave the salon. KayTee thought about the years that they had worked side by side. Sometimes Sandy stayed past five thirty to talk to her or Jill, but not very often.

Tonight, Sandy was dawdling. She spent an unusual amount of time packing up her supplies. KayTee wondered if Sandy was waiting for Beth and Jill to leave. Something was up. Would she make a scene over KayTee's hiring of Beth?

The clock above the door reached five-thirty. Jill was still busy with her last client, but as soon as Beth said goodbye and went out the door, Sandy said, "KayTee, when you get a minute, I want to talk to you out back." KayTee didn't want to lose Sandy. She was honest and reliable. They'd gotten along well. But, NO tenant was going to tell her who she could hire.

She finished off her last client. There was enough time before Amy Barcellos would arrive. So, KayTee went into the alley to face the dragon-fire that was going to come breathing out of Sandy's mouth over Beth's hiring. Sandy looked around to make sure no one was nearby to eavesdrop, then she did let her anger spew out. "KayTee Baker, how could you be so damn mean to Shon? All he wanted was good color. A simple thing. He's a nice guy. He is kind and helpful. He's really, really a nice guy." Sandy's eyes squinted. "What you said to him was just plain cruel."

KayTee was startled. This certainly wasn't what she'd expected to hear. "The guy from the gym? This is all about that silly boy from the gym?"

"Yes, it is. You know I work out there. I know the staff and Shon's a sweet kid. It bothers me that you were so rude to him. You had no reason to be so mean. All he wanted a foil weave. It wouldn't take long. You were just plain mean."

KayTee tried her best to sound cool and professional. "Sandy, this isn't your business. It is my salon and I don't want men in it. This is my decision to make, not yours. I'm not making any changes to the way I run things."

Sandy puffed her chest out and slid to the right, blocking KayTee from the backdoor to the salon. Sandy's posture wasn't quite menacing, but showed that she certainly wasn't giving up the fight. When she spoke, she wasn't loud enough for anyone in the alley other than KayTee to hear her, but her voice was harsh. "I work out in the gym three evenings a week. Shon is the kindest person, who works there. He's always ready to help with the equipment or spot us so we don't get hurt.

Pointing a finger at KayTee, Sandy raised her voice. "You are a bigot, KayTee Baker. You are a gender bigot! That is just as bad as being a black person bigot. You gave me a hard look this morning because my face reminded you I didn't want to work with black people. Well, I don't. They've scared me since I got beat-up by a big black girl when I was a little kid. And still, you saw that I was nice to Beth today. I can be nice." She pointed to herself. "I can. Even though she's tall I knew it wasn't her who beat me up." She didn't want to cry, but she was getting teary-eyed.

"You are no better than me, KayTee Baker. I don't know what some guy did to you once, but you should have gotten over it by now. It wasn't Shon who did it. The least you can do is be nice to him. Don't be such a goddamn bigot."

KayTee didn't know what to say. A bigot? Nobody, in her entire life, had ever accused her of being a bigot. She just stood there, her eyes getting bigger as she listened to what Sandy was saying. "If you don't want to do Shon's hair, I can do it. I'm not as good as you on foil weaves. So, he wants *you* to do his color. But I can if you won't." Sandy sniffed, wiggled her nose, and went on. "Jill could even do it. Besides, think about it the business opportunity. There are lots of other guys out there who want salons to do their cuts and color. Guys want style. It isn't 1980 anymore. It isn't 2000 either. It is time for you to catch up."

Almost a full minute ticked away with the two women

standing silently in the alley staring at each other. Then, KayTee nodded her head. "Okay," she said. "Okay. When you work out next time, tell Shon I said he could come in and I'll schedule his weave."

"You will?"

"Yes. I will. But I'm not changing the marquee, and I don't want him strutting around acting like some rooster in my shop. He has to act like an ordinary client."

"Thank you!" Sandy's face brightened and her teary eyes found their twinkle again. She looked at KayTee and asked, "We're okay?"

KayTee and Sandy went back inside the salon at just about the same time that Beth finished crossing the length of the parking lot and was back in the little park, waiting for the bus. She noticed that the parking lot was still quite full, but the old white guys and their chessboard were gone. Beth was anxious to get home to play with Joshua and to tell her mom about the day. She had a job in a pretty salon with flowery wallpaper and nice people. Soon she'd have the salon's work mastered and she would be able to accentuate clients' beauty in all the ways she'd learned at beauty school.

She looked across the cars to scan the mall as she had that morning. There was a toy store. On Friday, she'd buy something for Joshua. Her mother loved plants. There was a greenery shop with pretty ceramic pots in its window right next door to *Beauty Accentuated*.

Beth could make plans. First, she'd begin by helping her mom financially. Eventually, she'd buy a car. Reverend

Morgan's brother sang in the choir with her. He was a mechanic. If she asked him, he'd make sure she got the right car, one with a good engine and new tires. It could be warm burgundy, or emerald green, or a shimmery dark blue. Not white, silver or gold, she didn't want those. She wanted a pretty color for her car.

Just then, with the swish of air brakes and a squeaky glide of its door opening, the bus to the south end of town arrived. Bethlehem Jackson got on.

The Pot Spot

By Carolyn Barbre

Stash took his job quite seriously. The ten-pound tuxedo tomcat was so named because he sported one-half of a black mustache beneath his nose, on the left muzzle, but only white fur on the right. Stash lived in the Pot Spot, the end shop at the North Point Mall nearest Minor Street. Through the bullet-proof Plexiglas front window, shoppers could indeed see a colorful collection of pots of varying shapes and sizes. Some displayed beautiful bouquets, so that the Pot Spot was frequently mistaken for the floral shop housed over among the north-side shops. Many contained sprouted marijuana plants, growing tall and healthy in pots designed for that purpose—deep pots with numerous drainage holes.

The fifty-by seventy-five-foot space was structured so that the front fifty feet were squared off as the Pot Spot, while the back twenty-five housed the marijuana dispensary. Stash stood guard at the dispensary door. Customers would step inside and present their driver's license to the armed guard who read it into the computer as a permanent record. Stash would slip in behind the person or persons (no more than two at a time) and practically trip them as he wove his body between their moving feet. Then the guard pressed a button unlocking the door to the inner chamber where the cannabis goods were on display in glass cases. Stash would sit by the door, waiting patiently to escort the shopper(s) back to the street.

It seemed that folks in poor rural areas were shocked at the very idea that citizens could be 'rolling reefers and smoking dope,' as they anachronistically referred to the legendary mood-soothing weed. But not so the septuagenarian sisters, Iris and Matilda (aka Matty). Iris had researched the subject and decided to buy some cannabis-infused edibles to help lower her perpetually high blood pressure, and hopefully, the creeping glaucoma that was stealing her eyesight.

Matilda was bent over like a pretzel, due to osteoporosis. She was a lifelong sugar junky, likely the precursor of her false teeth and thinning bone structure. She needed a cane to walk anywhere and preferred a wheeled walker with a seat. But such mobility aids were difficult to maneuver in small shops. Matilda consumed opioids morning and evening. She said they soothed her chronic pain from rheumatoid arthritis. Iris hoped to get her sister off addictive drugs and onto non-addictive marijuana. She thought that cannabis-infused candy might do the trick.

After weeks of rain, finally a bright sunny day inspired Iris to get in her vintage VW bug and tool on over to the North Point Mall to check out the Pot Spot. She decided to circle the block before pulling into the parking lot. Iris noticed a large black-and-white cat seemingly standing guard at the Pot Spot's rear entrance. Cat lover that she was, she immediately pulled into the first available space, locked the bug, and headed back toward the cat. Stash stood, his tail held high, and rubbed against Iris' legs.

"What a fine, handsome fellow you are," Iris enthused while stroking the feline's back and scratching his ears. Stash did not purr. He could only offer a scratchy, undecipherable meow. "Oh, I'm sorry," Iris commiserated. She wondered if it was genetic or the result of some injury. Iris pulled open the glass door to the dispensary and stepped inside with Stash at her heels. At the guard's instruction, Iris pulled out her driver's license and the guard read it into the computer. A plate of delicious-looking cookies sat on a corner of the desk.

Seeing the old woman look at the plate of cookies, the guard said, "Feel free to help yourself."

"Oh, thank you," Iris said, picking up a big chocolate chip treat. Knowing it was more than she would eat, she asked if it was okay to give some to the kitty.

"He won't eat it," said the guard. "He only eats cheese and scrambled eggs. A lacto-ovo he is—won't hardly even eat meat."

Iris wondered if that accounted for his barely audible, scratchy meow. The security guard buzzed her into the retail shop. Iris pulled out her wallet and extracted a hundred-dollar bill.

"What do you recommend?" she asked the clerk behind the left-side counter. "My lungs are shot, so it has to be edibles."

"No problem," replied the clerk. He recommended Chong's Choice, a white-chocolate bar coated on one side with cinnamon crunch cereal. "One of our best sellers," he said. Iris took one Chong's Choice and two dark-chocolate bars, already scored to break into 20 sections at 5 mg THC each, the recommended dosage. Warnings stated that there was nothing to be gained by taking higher doses. No worries—taking the proper dosage of any drug was virtually sacrosanct to seniors on meds.

❧

As Christmas neared, Iris decided to give one of the chocolate bars as her present to Matilda. When she dropped by her sister's house and handed her the cardboard-packaged chocolate bar, Matilda whooped with delight, clearly already aware of what the package contained. She thanked Iris and tossed the candy bar on the top of a small bookcase that stood against the living room wall next to the kitchen doorway. Iris assumed her sister was keeping it out of reach of her two little dogs, a Lhasa Apso and a miniature poodle.

❧

Come spring, Iris asked Matilda if she'd consumed her special candy bar yet.

"I can't find it," Matilda confessed.

"What do you mean you can't find it? I watched you toss it up on that little bookcase by your kitchen doorway."

"I think maybe my housekeeper took it," Matilda replied. "She's a drug addict, so much so that she lost her hearing due to her abuse of drugs."

"Why on earth would you employ a deaf drug addict as a housekeeper?"

"Because she needs the money, and she's very sweet."

"And apparently, she's a thieving drug addict. Is she stealing your opioids?"

"No, I left some on the bathroom counter, and she never touched them."

"Druggies know a trap when they see one," Iris said, dumbfounded by her sister's naiveté. "I just called to see if you would like to come with me to the Pot Spot, the marijuana dispensary at the North Point Mall."

Matilda complained that she didn't have any money, which Iris knew was simply a matter of priorities. Her sister had money for a housekeeper, and for having her hair done. She also had her dogs professionally groomed every month. Her husband ran the family business he'd inherited from his father, a very profitable enterprise, and he gave Matty a generous allowance.

"It's my gas, and I'll buy you lunch, but you have to buy your own drugs. I'll pick you up at 10:30 tomorrow morning if you want to come along," Iris said.

"I'll see if I can dig up some change," Matilda said, sounding doubtful.

❧

Iris putted into Matilda's driveway a little after 10 a.m. She parked the bug and went to her sister's front door where she knocked and started the puppies yapping. Matilda shouted for her to come on in, which Iris did, pushing the puppies out of her way. Matilda was searching for her collapsible cane, which she found next to her oversized recliner. She grabbed a couple of bottles of water out of the fridge and put them in her purse.

They made their way out to the VW, and Iris opened the passenger-side door. Matilda asked Iris to hold her purse. Then she maneuvered herself into the shotgun seat. Iris couldn't believe how heavy the purse was. "What have you got in here? It weighs like ten pounds!"

"Yeah, I guess it is kind of heavy," Matilda agreed.

"You decided the purse was stylish, regardless of how unsuited it is to your needs, didn't you?" Iris accused. "Remember what I told you when we went through that chic little shop that carried some very smart-looking thigh-high boots?" Making air-quotes, Iris said, "It's gauche for septuagenarians to wear thigh-high boots."

"I forget that I'm getting old. It just seems like everyone else is getting younger."

"I know, sweetie." Iris handed the purse back to Matilda, walked around the VW and got into the driver's seat. *We aren't getting old. We're already old.* She put the key in the ignition while Matilda folded her cane, stuffed it down beside her leg, and pulled two rolls of quarters and two rolls of dimes from her purse.

Looking askance, Iris sat quiet for a few moments. "Please tell me you aren't planning on paying for drugs with rolls of coins."

"It's all I had," Matilda whined.

"Give it to me," Iris said as she pulled a twenty and a ten from her wallet. She handed the bills to Matilda and dumped the rolled coins into a slot in the dashboard. At the same time, she could see, as Matilda clicked open her cloth change-purse, that it was stuffed with bills. Iris just shook her head.

"Seriously, you don't want anyone thinking you broke into your grandchildren's piggy banks to pay for your drugs, do you?"

Matilda started laughing, and Iris joined in. "We aren't supposed to get the giggles until we partake of some form of cannabis," she chortled.

"I picked some succulents, and I don't want to just have them meandering about my yard. I want to put them in some pretty pots," Matilda said, as if cannabis was of no interest. "Oh, I have to tell you. I went through the stack of stuff on my bookcase with my housekeeper, and we found the missing candy bar. I even had a little taste of one square."

So Matty won't be shopping for any cannabis products today, or maybe ever. There went Iris's hope of changing her sister's choice of addictive vs. nonaddictive drugs.

Matilda purchased three attractive pots that left her bill-filled coin purse noticeably thinner. The clerk and Iris carried the containers to the VW and put them in the trunk. "As long as we're here, let's see what the Pot Spot dispensary has in stock," Iris said.

They made their way to the Pot Spot's alley door and went through the security check, with Stash, the tuxedo tomcat, at their heels. Iris petted the supercilious critter, while Matilda struggled to find her expired license.

"You know me," said Iris to the guard. "I can vouch for

my sister." The guard pushed the buzzer and Iris pulled the security door open. Matilda followed her. The Pot Spot's stock of cannabis-infused sweets was pitiful. The display cases were almost empty.

"Looks like this place has really caught on," Iris sighed. Each of the sisters paid $40 for a ten-count bag of cookies, strawberry flavored for Matilda and lemon for Iris. As they departed the marijuana dispensary, Stash stood up and started accompanying the women out the door. He apparently inadvertently knocked Matilda's cane, so that it collapsed and Matty along with it. Her humped-over body rolled once and then she flattened out on her back, with noticeable cracking noises. Looking dazed and confused, she rose up onto her elbows, rotated her head, and concluded that she had been divinely healed. *Praise God, and His emissary, Stash!*

"Good heavens! Are you okay?" Iris gasped. "Should I call for EMTs?"

Stash stepped up on Matty's mostly prone figure and began to purr a real purr, and a very self-satisfied purr. Matilda sat up, then stood up with a hand from Iris, and dusted herself off. "Look at me. I'm better than okay!"

"Yes, I can see," Iris said, tears streaming down her cheeks as she gave her sister a big hug.

"How about I buy lunch today at the Doughnut Hole," Matty suggested.

Always with the sweets. But she loved her sister. "Sounds like a plan," Iris replied, and the pair practically skipped off across the mall parking lot.

The Florist Shop

By Peyton Ellas

This Diary Fragment Was Found After the Disaster That Destroyed the North Point Mall

Everything would be fine if the Old One would leave. She started appearing a week ago and since then the meat food hasn't been left out anymore. We are not as stupid as They think. We deduced the connection immediately. In the food's place are the tablets. Long ago, past the time of remembering, we developed an aversion to sweet, but these are not sweet. I saw others partake and die. Therefore, I have not partaken. We are not as stupid as They think. The ones who died were not stupid. Brave.

The Very Young One left yellow flowers in the indoor trash. There are a lot of flowers here with us, mostly in cold caves or very high up. We are surrounded by floral smells, but most of them not connected to edible. If the flowers don't go with other humans after a few days, They have always taken them outside in the back. To the bin beyond, some say, but it's not quite clear. This place smells sweet (disgusting), but is a good temperature, and the colony has been here since before the time of remembering. Hundreds of generations perhaps. The flowers in the indoor trash bin along with a little soap from the bottle in the kitchen, are the only reasons I haven't starved to death or succumbed. The tablets are very tempting. They have something about them more like the meat that used to be left out for the felines than the sweet of the cold caves. The flowers are not much better than ordinary paper. We used to lick the glue in the seams of the paper cups, but they have been sealed up in plastic bins we can't get into. There's usually plentiful food we can find in any domicile, but since the Old One started boxing and sealing and spraying and leaving tablets, things have gone from bad to worse.

The Old One yelled at the Very Young One. Since that happened, there aren't any more flowers in the indoor trash. Several females are carrying eggs ready to hatch. The females are naturally not feeding, but what will their young do?

I tried out my wings. They were, predictably, weak. I glided but could not get far. I had thought I might be able to make it to the bin beyond, but it doesn't appear possible.

They had the Man come again. He sealed up more cracks with a foam that dried so you couldn't see it and smells like their most disgusting flowers. What are they trying to do to us? Don't they know we're here? Don't they know what they are doing to us? Several hundred are trapped and feared dead.

The Very Young One left flowers in the trash again. Bless her! They had recently been removed from water, so we had our thirst slaked. It had been more than a week, and several of the younger ones expired,Which made a satisfying meal, so all was not lost. But water! And a little nibble at something delicate and floriferous. We don't prefer to eat our expired young. They are not preferred. We did it to survive.

What do I spend my days doing? Sleeping. Wedging myself into the tiniest space. There is more space now that so many have died. But yesterday there was a large hatching. The little ones ate the legs off their mothers and nibbled at my wings. I felt compelled to let them, even though I didn't care for it. There wasn't much else in their reach to eat. I had thought I could still mate with a few of the females, once their eggs were hatched and dropped, but the females haven't called. Perhaps being legless is not a good thing. I don't know, really. Of course, I don't want to be legless. But we males have a different lifestyle and a different role. We need our legs more than the females. It's irritating, really. I have a little energy after all. But it won't work without them calling me.

No more flowers for days. It is hard to pass by the tablets. I chose different routes, but the tablets move around, or there are more of them. I don't know. It's hard to think. I am so hungry. It drives me towards nibbling the tablets. But I will not. I can resist. I am fully grown. I must find females during the nights I have left. How long will the Old One live? They seem to live longer than we do. I would like to nibble her legs off. She is not here when it is dark. We only see her when we are rousing from slumber and then she leaves. I see her sometimes as I am ready for slumber, just arriving. But it's not possible to nibble anything when slumber calls. Some of us do not make it back to our day spaces. If we try to do too much in the mornings, we just slumber in the light and that's it. I know some who in the past stayed out in the light on purpose because they couldn't stand the idea of being consumed by the rest of us. I am not so selfish. I would like to die peacefully in my day space and then let them all have at me. But without the tablet poison. They would not partake with the poison in me. We can smell it on each other.

Big night! Many females calling. I am exhausted and hungry. Everywhere I turn, there is only tablet.

Tablet, tablet, tablet. In my dreams. NO.

Should we have left when the ants did?

One who may have been my direct brother succumbed. He couldn't help it. I understand. But the activities of the other night give me more determination to hold out. How many females? I lost track. But that may be hundreds of offspring. If only I had a good meal to celebrate. How many days since I ate anything besides the bits of soap in the kitchen? All the good food is in jars or the large white box that has the heat out the back (how nice that was when I was first born!) The felines wail at night. They suffer too. The Old One is cruel.

The Very Young One left a banana on the counter. Lovely. We took turns. Youngest first. I did get a meager meal out of it. Not enough.

The Old One yelled at the Very Young One again. The Man returned and sprayed. I only heard about it from a few youngsters who hadn't yet started their slumber when it all happened. I am finding it more difficult to stay awake. I rise only for a few hours each night. I haven't heard any females calling in days.

Others came from a different colony. We hadn't had a mixing since I was very young, a week or so old. It was delightful and frightening at the same time. They told of mass slaughter. Some kind of food that seemed like a gift but the young ones never grew to their next phase. I shudder. At least I am fully formed. And let's face it, I haven't got much time in my natural life. But the young ones! It's tragic. Most of those who arrived from the other colony are old. But the younger males from our colony fell onto the few new females from theirs with gusto. I held back.

I am thinking of eating my fill of the tablets and calling it good. I saw several of the females from the new colony do that. What a waste! After our males used energy to mate with them. Disgusting. That gives me resolve. I may be old. I may not mate the way I used to. (Oh, those glory days!) But I can show the others how we should behave. How we must behave. Resist! My internal parts are grinding, and I am in such pain. But I will resist!

The Very Young One left BUTTERED breadcrumbs behind the white metal box. This cannot be a trick. Can it? Breadcrumbs have always been my favorites, and buttered? I was in a troubled state between sleep and wake and here come her fingers, long and white with those claw things on the end that They all have. And the breadcrumbs showered down, right on top of me and the dozens of others crammed snugly in with me. There was general rousing, then a good feed. I held back at first, mistrustful. Everyone was saying, "angel," "angel," "angel." As if they knew what that meant. It's a general word used whenever a human leaves the trash open or the meat out or doesn't wipe a spill. We have a lot of angels in a typical colony. But the Very Young One is the most loved.

I held back at first. But not for long. Buttered breadcrumbs.

The angel you most love is the doom you accept. I feel remarkably fine, given it all. I made it to 180 days. Almost a full life term. New young ones were hatched today, and the word was spread to them quickly. DON'T TRUST THE BUTTERED BREADCRUMBS. DON'T TRUST THE VERY YOUNG ONE.

Bless you all. Long live the colony.

THANK YOU

Thank you for taking the time to read *Tulare Kings Writers Present Tales from the Strip Mall*. Please consider writing a short review on GoodReads or Amazon. It would mean a great deal to the authors.

ABOUT THE AUTHORS

A. K. Antheson

A. K. Antheson was writing before he actually learned to write, creating songs and stories he later committed to paper. He has written poetry, a book of short stories, as well as a novella. He is currently working on a fantasy adventure and a collection of autobiographical stories. Antheson has been a resident of the Central Valley of California for forty years. He may be reached at magicdragonwriter@yahoo.com.

Julie Appelbaum

Julie Appelbaum was born and raised in the California Bay Area and earned her Bachelor of Arts degree in English Literature at U. C. Berkeley. She earned a Master's of Public Administration from the University of Puget Sound. She had extensive work experience as a teacher, professor, and manager in mental health. She has travelled extensively and has many interesting experiences to share through her poetry.

Appelbaum has always loved literature. She believes poetry is the essence of a dream captured in words, and has been writing poetry for seven years. Her debut book, *Poems of Light, Hope, and Joy*, is available at amazon.com. She is working on her second book of poetry, *Thriving in the Thicket*.

Carolyn Barbre

Carolyn Barbre has lived in Springville, California since the late 1990s. She wrote profiles about people of interest for the weekly *Tule River Times* for a year. She free-lanced for the *Fresno Bee* before signing on as the City Beat reporter for the *Lindsay Gazette*. Barbre was then employed by the City of Lindsay to fill a new position as "City Arts Coordinator."

In 2002 Barbre was awarded 1st Place for "Environmental/Ag Reporting" from the California Newspaper Publishers Association (CNPA) She placed second for "Public Service" in 2003 from CNPA, and was a Blue Ribbon Finalists for Editorial Comment. She also garnered 2003, 2004 and 2005 George F. Gruner awards for Meritorious Public Service in Journalism.

Judith Bixby Boling

A native Californian, Judith Bixby Boling has been writing short stories and essays since elementary school. She utilized her research and writing skills while employed as a paralegal and construction specifier. Boling and her husband share a love of American history, which led them to become Civil War reenactors and living historians. While she is usually seen depicting a Northern woman, on occasion you may find her on the battlefield portraying a woman disguised as a Union cannoneer.

Boling is the author of the *Priscilla Saga* series. Her books are available at The Book Garden in Exeter, California and www.amazon.com/author/judithbixbyboling.

Readers are invited to connect with Judith Bixby Boling on Amazon, Facebook Goodreads, and Twitter, and contact her at courtstpress@gmail.com.

Liam Boling

Ten-year-old Liam Boling enjoys reading and writing, as well as playing video games. He collaborated with his grandmother, Judith Bixby Boling, to write *Chuckie's Toy Store.*

Roger Boling

Roger Boling wrote parody fiction in high school. After college he worked for an engineering firm that imported surveying and engineering equipment from Japan and other Asian countries. Boling was tasked with revising the technical manuals that had been literally translated into English by the manufacturer ("take right wrench hand turn left) to improve readability for their customers.

Subsequent to retirement, Boling began writing in earnest. He is currently writing two works of fiction. *Velma June's Discount Coffin Shop* is his first published work.

Newell Bringhurst

Newell G. Bringhurst is an independent scholar and Professor Emeritus of History and Political Science at College of the Sequoias.

He is the author/editor of thirteen books. His most recent are *The Mormon Quest of the Presidency: Eleven Mormons who Ran for President from 1844 to 2012* (2011), co-authored with Craig L. Foster; and *The Mormon Church and Blacks: A Documentary History* co-edited with Matthew l. Harris (2015).

Bringhurst has also written on Visalia/Tulare County history, his most important work, *Visalia's Fabulous Fox: A Theater History* (1999). He is currently completing *College of the Sequoias: A Century of Excellence, 1926-2020,* slated for publication in 2020.

"Ruby's Antique-Pawn Shoppe" represents Bringhurst's first attempt at fiction writing. He expresses sincere gratitude to those members of the local writers' community who encouraged and aided him, in particular, Judith Bixby Boling, and members of the Packwood Writers critique group.

Ronn Couillard

Ronn Couillard has worked in the criminal justice system in California since 1968. He began as a deputy district attorney for Los Angeles County. In June, 1980, he moved to Visalia and served as a deputy district attorney for Tulare County. He was appointed to the Tulare County Superior Court in 1987. After retiring in 2007, he continued as an assigned judge until September, 2016. In the past forty-eight years, he has both prosecuted and presided over, all types of felony matters, including numerous murder cases. He and his wife, Charlotte, reside in Visalia. They have four grown children and seven grandchildren.

Couillard is the author of three books: *MURDER IN VISALIA: The Coin Dealer Killer, THE FRAME-UP: A Murder in Visalia,* and *STORIES OF MURDER AND MIRTH.*

Peyton Ellas

Peyton Ellas lives in Springville. Her work has appeared in *Onthebus, Gihon River Review, Southern Sierra Messenger, the debaser,* and other places. Her first book, *Gardening with California Native Plants: Inland, Foothill and Central Valley Gardens,* was published in February 2019.

Gloria Getman

Gloria Getman, author of the *Deena Powers Mystery* series, spent 25 years as a registered nurse before following her bliss into writing fiction. She grew up in Southern California, graduated from California State University Bakersfield and lives in Exeter California. Her work has been featured in local publications as well as Yesterday's Magazette and Reminisce Extra. She placed third in the Lillian Dean First Page Competition for a novel at the Central Coast Writer's Conference. A few of her short stories can be found in the anthology, *Leaves from the Valley Oak.* She is a member of Tulare-Kings Writers, plus San Joaquin and Central Coast chapters of Sisters in Crime. Her books are available at the Book Garden in Exeter and at Amazon.com, either as a paperback or ebook. You can find her on Facebook and at gloriagetman.blogspot.com.

Lois Innis

I love Southern California where I was born and my husband and I raised our family. The near-by mountains lured our clan to Tulare County. I volunteered at World Ag Expo in Tulare, California for many years.

My husband was diagnosed with Alzheimer's in 2009. I began writing in order to share anecdotes and insights with people just discovering a loved one has a dementia.

Shirley A. Blair Keller

Journaling daily led Shirley A. Blair Keller to storytelling and art.

Keller's storytelling interest led to creating ceramic masks, because faces tell stories. Turquoise, her favorite color, became the acrylic base coat on items she repurposed. She fell deeply in love with one dot at a time, turning trash into happy art pieces. Keller worked in the workshop of Silvia and Efrain Fuentes, artisans of excellence, in Oaxaca, Mexico. They inspired patience in Keller to explore dots on recent favorites: used hubcaps, skill saws and old mirrors.

She designed Ink Quilts on a kitchen counter to go with her memoir: *But What about the Children? Diversity is Life: A Memoir,* published in 2019.

Connect with Keller at www.1stsaturdaytr.com and www.sbaircreativeplay.blogspot.com.

You may contact her at sblairkeller@sbcglobal.net.

Janet LeBaron

Janet LeBaron has created a life of adventure: healer, entrepreneur and mystic. From owning a mussel farm in New Zealand, to working on muscles as a massage therapist, she developed a latent ability as a business intuitive. Working with advertising agencies, she creates original innovations to generate new streams of revenue and client loyalty. In addition, she gives classes at Chambers of Commerce regarding changes in patent law, the 'America Invents' Act.

Her desire to help also flows into assisting others to perfect their soul's journey in life. *Logic, Love and God*© will be published in early spring 2020. *The Metaphysical Shoppe* is her first work of fiction.

LeBaron lives with her beloved husband, Don, and can be contacted at jl@intuitiveinnovation.com.

Elizabeth Morse

Elizabeth Morse is seven years old and in the second grade at Riverview Elementary School, in Fresno, California. She likes to help her GG make stuff for dinner. She likes when she and GG come up with ideas to write books. Elizabeth says when GG writes about her in a book it makes her feel happy.

Irene Morse

Irene Morse lives in Visalia, California with her husband, Gary Benjamin. They have a lovely, blended, and rapidly growing family. When not writing, she likes to travel to places where she can make new friends, try new food, and be amazed. Morse likes to read, cook, and dig in the dirt, but most of all she loves to play with her great-grandchildren. Her adventure series, *The Perilous Peregrinations of Penelope Pipsqueak*, includes children with superpowers who may resemble these Greats. Contact her at irene@ingramct.com.

McKenzie Morse

McKenzie Morse is eleven years old, and attends sixth grade, in Fresno, California. In addition to liking all of her classes, she loves sports. She likes when her GG writes about her or when she can help with her stories, because it makes her feel very special. McKenzie says that GG takes the ideas she gives her and creates magnificent art pieces.

Steve Pastis

Steve Pastis, moved from Orange County to Visalia in 2006. Pastis has written for the *Valley Voice, The Good Life, Greek Accent, Farm News, Custom Boat & Engine, Baseball Cards, Circus, Rock Fever, Occidental Magazine, Destination Visalia, South Valley Networking, The Hellenic*

Calendar, Cool and Strange Music, and *Gargoyle.* His first short story collection, *Fables for the Clarinet,* is available on

Sylvia Ross

Sylvia Ross is the author of *Acorns and Abalone,* a book of poetry, art, and short stories; *Acts of Kindness, Acts of Contrition, East of the Great Valley,* and *Ilsa Rohe, Parsing Vengeance,* fact-based novels; *Coming to Completion,* a book of personal essays; and also some children's books. Born in Southern California, she attended parochial schools, later working as a cell painter at Walt Disney Studio. After she married, she and her husband settled in the Central Valley and raised a family. She earned an honor's degree from Fresno State University and taught school in Porterville for a number of years. She now lives in rural Exeter where she continues to write and do artwork.

Jacque Summers

Jacque Summers moved to Visalia in 2009. She earned a degree in Creative Writing and English from Southern New Hampshire University and has eight years experience as a teacher.

She has published two nonfiction chapter books: *Disgusting Jobs in Modern America* (Capstone), *Escaping a POW Camp* (Momentum). She ghost wrote *Abraham Lincoln and the Forest of Little Pigeon Creek* (AmeriTales) and *Sitting Bull and the Roaring Winds of the Great Plains* (AmeriTales). Summers has been published in Ladybug Magazine with the story, *The Basketweaver* and won the SCBWI 2006 Writer's Day Contest for her picture book manuscript *Pirate Princess* and her middle grade novel *Spartan Son.*

Authors not providing an email address may be contacted at
tularekingswritersca@gmail.com

Made in the
USA
Columbia, SC